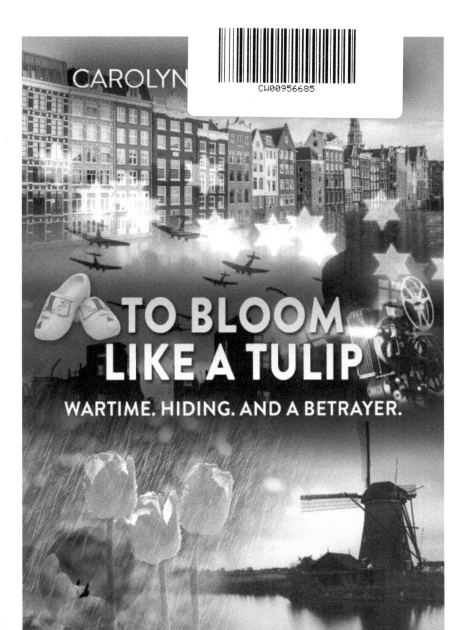

CAROLYN

TO BLOOM LIKE A TULIP

WARTIME. HIDING. AND A BETRAYER.

TO BLOOM LIKE A TULIP

First edition. October 22, 2024.

ISBN: 979-8227742834

Written by Carolyn Summer Quinn.

"Deep in their roots, all flowers keep the light."
—Theodore Roethke

"Whoever saves a life saves the world entire."
—The Talmud

Dedication

In memory of two of the most phenomenal people I've ever known, the volunteers who ran the Scotch Plains-Fanwood Summer Music Theater Workshop in Scotch Plains, New Jersey, Manya Ungar and Judy Cole. They not only gave of their time to introduce hundreds of kids to the world of the theater but did it all for free.

BRAVA!

"Oranje boven."
Translation:
"Orange above all!"
A classic saying inspired by the Dutch royal family, whose surname is Oranje-Nassau, and a popular expression of resistance during World War II.

Chapter One

May 1940
Amsterdam, The Netherlands

———⊶⊶⊷———

MAY 10, 1940, SHOULD have been an ordinary day but it wasn't. It turned out to be anything but. The people of the Netherlands awoke to find themselves under a ferocious attack.

It began with a roar early in the morning, at 4:30 AM, of all times, and before the sun had even had a chance to come up. Thirteen-year-old Rika Spranger, along with her older brothers, Kees, fourteen, fifteen-year-old Henk, and their father, Julius, were rudely awakened by the sound of what seemed like hundreds of planes flying over Amsterdam. Hundreds! The racket of all those flying airplane motors was nothing less than terrible.

The implication of what it probably meant for Holland was even worse.

Rika rushed to the window of their apartment to see what was happening. Her father, coming into the front room right behind her, yelled at her to for heaven's sake get away from the windows in case a bomb hit their building and shattered the glass.

A bomb?

Rika shivered, though it wasn't really all that cold in the apartment, and moved away from the window as fast as she could, almost taking off from the ground and flying, or so it seemed, as she made her way into the dining room.

Her brother Henk turned on the radio. It wasn't long before the family heard the Dutch government's terrifying broadcast.

"Germany has invaded the Netherlands! Remain calm. Follow instructions by the authorities," was the way it began, and the lives of the Spranger family would never be the same again.

Not long after the first frightening announcement came another. "Beware of German paratroopers!" It was surreal. Unimaginable. The Nazis weren't just invading their country on the ground. They were also dropping soldiers from planes, with parachutes, to infiltrate the country by way of the air!

The news got even crazier. According to another announcement, there were also Nazis storming into the country dressed as members of the *Dutch* armed forces, or in farmer's clothes, or as clergymen. Some German soldiers were even on the march or dropped out of the planes with their parachutes dressed *as nuns*!

Everyone was warned to stay inside, and the Sprangers didn't have to be told that twice.

"You're not going to school today," Julius told his sons and daughter.

"What some people will do to get out of school," Kees tried to joke. It made Rika give way to a bit of a smile, but not Henk or their father. This was no laughing matter, but Kees always did what he could to try and lighten things up.

Outside there came the sound of a metallic crash. A building near their Amsterdam neighborhood must have gotten hit. Rika let out a wail.

"German *bastaards*," Henk muttered.

"This," said Julius needlessly, "is not good for us."

His children already knew it.

He meant, in particular, that it was a terrible development not just due to the fact that they were Dutch, and their country was being invaded, but also because they were Jewish.

The Sprangers weren't the kind of Jewish that spent every Sabbath day in the synagogue. They were the non-observant type and showed up at the temple only on the holidays, if they went there at all, but still, their personal particulars weren't going to matter to the Nazis, and they knew it. The family were members of a religion that was hated with a passion by the screeching Nazi leader, Adolf Hitler. And that was that. This would almost certainly mean a ton of trouble for them down the road.

It had already happened to the Jews in Germany, not to mention Austria and Poland. The Nazis were making the lives of Jewish people impossible in every country they had the nerve to overtake.

Over the last few years the Sprangers' city of Amsterdam had been inundated with Jewish refugees from Germany who had fled to Holland to escape Nazi persecution. There were all kinds of prohibitions against the Jews in Germany, enacted by Hitler and his like-minded, hate filled cabinet. Jews couldn't hold down certain jobs, marry non-Jews, go to certain public places, and more. Jewish children could not even go to school with non-Jewish German ones!

The German Jewish refugees had come to the Netherlands in the hopes that their country would remain neutral in the event of another war, just as it had stayed neutral during World War One, the last one. Hitler seemed to be itching to start trouble.

Well, that expectation was over as of right now, Julius thought, shaking his balding head. We're not neutral. They're invading us!

If only, Rika thought, they'd gone to America with their mother, Florentine, as she heard another bomb exploding somewhere outside. What a stupid move it was to have remained behind! Now here they were, a divided family, on two different sides of the Atlantic Ocean, *and* they were being invaded by the Nazis.

Yet who could know in advance that *this* would ever happen?

Florentine's father, Rika's grandfather, had lived in Brooklyn, New York, where he owned a flower shop, from sometime in the 1920s onwards. He had died there several months earlier around the time of Hanukkah.

Florentine had taken her two youngest children, Verena and Willem, along with her on a ship to the United States, hoping to go there and settle her father's estate as fast as she possibly could. The family thought it would be a fine adventure for Verena and Willem to go to school in America for about six months or so before sailing back home to Holland.

The estate had taken longer to settle than Florentine had anticipated it would, however. Rika had a feeling that her mother and siblings weren't going to be returning to Amsterdam now. Maybe not ever. Not if the Nazis took over.

There was another explosion from somewhere not far away. It rattled the windows of their apartment.

"Come," Kees shouted over the noise outside to the others, "let's get our rear ends under the table. It will be better for us to stay there if the windows get shattered."

Rika could only wonder as she joined the others crouching under the table.

How was any of this *happening?*

⎯⎯⎯⎯➤◉⎯⎯⎯⎯

THE NETHERLANDS WAS defeated in only five days.

The Germans won.

They always seemed to win.

Now *they* were in charge of their country.

There was more horrible news. Queen Wilhelmina hadn't even lasted for the full five days of the battle before she fled. It was absolutely maddening to the Dutch. Her Majesty got onto a British destroyer only three days after the first Nazis crossed the border. By May 13th, she was gone.

The Queen's daughter, Princess Juliana, and her husband and two children fled, too. Somewhere safe. Or, at least, safer than this.

So the royal family had managed to get out, but the rest of the population got stuck here? It wasn't fair. Everyone said so. It didn't pay to concentrate on any of that, since a fact was a fact, but the idea rankled so many of the good Dutch people who were loyal to the crown, though it didn't seem to bother the pro-Nazis.

When Rika mentioned it to her father, he said he was very disappointed in the Queen for leaving, too, but added, "What do you think would have happened to her if the Nazis managed to capture her? I wouldn't have wanted to see her imprisoned. Or worse, shot. Would you?"

Rika admitted that no, she certainly would not have liked *that*.

But still.

Before their country capitulated completely, the royals weren't the only ones who tried to flee. Many people headed toward the ports, hoping to also get on a ship, any kind of ship, to England, or someplace else, to anywhere, really, it didn't matter where they wound up, as long as it wasn't another country occupied by Nazis.

A few made it. Most didn't.

The Sprangers waited a day or two before they decided to try. They managed to get to the seaport, hoping to board any vessel they could.

"Let's hope," Julius said to Henk, Kees and Rika, "that we can get out of here and join your mother, sister and brother in Brooklyn. Take only what you can carry and let's go!"

It sounded like a fabulous idea to Rika as she quickly packed a few items of clothing and other items in a small suitcase. To go to America and be with their mother, Verena and Willem again! It sounded like a dream.

Unfortunately, when they managed to get to the port, thousands of other people had the exact same idea of fleeing the country. The few ships that were sailing away could not accommodate them all.

The Sprangers had to turn around and go home.

Rika's dream didn't come true.

Chapter Two

May 14, 1940
Brooklyn, New York

FLORENTINE SPRANGER, the wife of Julius and mother of Kees, Henk, Rika, as well as Verena and Willem, was glued to the radio again in her late father's front parlor in Bay Ridge, Brooklyn.

Florentine had rarely been away from the radio since the news first aired on May 10th about the Nazi invasion of the Netherlands. She was living from news broadcast to news broadcast. If only there was a station that ran them continuously, but there wasn't. All kinds of silly shows came on in between the latest war updates from Europe, driving her half mad.

It was a catastrophe! The Netherlands was supposed to stay neutral! Wasn't it?

Well, come to think of it, obviously not.

The rest of her immediate family was over there.

If the Netherlands capitulated, they might not be able to get out. They would be trapped.

In a Nazi occupied zone.

And they were Jewish.

She was startled when the doorbell rang. At first, when she got up to answer it, she thought it might be Celeste Mancini, the woman who worked at the flower shop her father had owned and that Florentine still hadn't managed to sell off.

It wasn't Celeste.

It was a delivery boy from Western Union.

"Telegram for Mrs. Florentine Spranger," he said cheerfully.

"That's me." Florentine signed for it.

Once the boy left, she dreaded opening it. There had been Nazi German paratroopers landing all over the place in Holland. Nazis in Dutch uniforms, infiltrating. Bombings. Warfare.

What was the reason for this telegram? Had one of the members of her family been killed?

Or maybe even more than one?

It was a nightmare.

The Germans had already started the war even before Florentine's father died and she had decided to take her two youngest along with her to settle his affairs in Brooklyn. She and Julius had thought it would be better for her to go to the United States, handle everything, and then sail back, rather than having the entire family uprooted.

It made sense, then. Julius owned a bookstore business. The three older children were lyceum students. It was for the sake of not interrupting their education that this decision had been made, and now Florentine was ready to kick herself over it.

What a lot of nonsense! Leaving four family members in a country that was at risk of being invaded simply for the sake of hanging onto the business and not transferring the children out of their school!

They should have known better. Hitler invaded Poland in 1939, and England and France declared war on Germany over it.

And just because the Netherlands had been neutral during World War One didn't really guarantee a damned thing.

Of course Hitler would want to get his hands on it. Holland's western border was on the ocean. He and his ilk would want access to that just in case he wanted to send his Navy off to invade anyplace else, like England. He'd had his army march into France, Belgium and Luxembourg on the tenth day of May, too. Luxembourg wasn't on the ocean, of course, but France, Belgium and the Netherlands all were. It wasn't just the Netherlands that the creep wanted.

And the ocean had to be crossed if Hitler wanted to take over England next.

The *bastaard!* No doubt he would want to control the whole world next.

With trembling hands and a sigh, Florentine opened the telegram.

It was a relief to see that it was from her husband, Julius. That meant he, at least, was alive.

It read:

———— ◉ ————

STAY THERE. DON'T sell.
> *Keep business and house.*
> *Will try to get there with K H and R.*
> *Julius*

———— ◉ ————

SO THEY WERE ALL STILL breathing. What a relief!

But how would Julius ever manage to emigrate now, of all times, with the other three children?

She already knew the answer. He wouldn't.

———— ◉ ————

"YOU'RE UP AT BAT, REENIE!" Celeste Mancini's daughter Barbara called out.

School had ended for the day, and Verena and Willem, aged eleven and nine, were playing stickball in the school playground with some of their new American friends. It wasn't a real bat that Verena was holding. It was the handle of a mop. Brooklyn kids had long learned how to make do with what they had in order to have a good time.

Florentine had finally pushed herself to leave her father's house on 84th Street to go in search of her youngest children.

No, wait, she said to herself as she glanced at the children and their game. She had to stop thinking of it as her father's house. It wasn't his. Not anymore, anyway. It was hers, now. Julius wanted her to remain there, and that seemed to be an excellent idea, especially at this point.

Selling the house and the flower shop had turned out to be an impossible feat to accomplish anyway. America wasn't fully recovered from the Great Depression yet and it had proven difficult to find a buyer for either the house or the shop.

Her father had done her a great service. She had a paid-for home and a good business, the flower shop, which gave her a way of supporting herself and Verena and Willem.

Oh, not "Verena" and "Willem," she remembered now, as Tommy Mancini said, "You're up next, Billy!" Her children currently called themselves by the American nicknames "Reenie" and "Billy." It was hard for Florentine to get used to the monikers, but she was trying.

"Reenie and Billy," she called out now.

"Hi, Mom," Reenie replied with a smile and a big wave. She had been in public school for months now and had almost lost her Dutch accent.

Florentine wanted to call the two of them over and tell them about the telegram. She believed they'd be thrilled when they heard the news that they'd be staying in America. Neither one of them really wanted to return to Amsterdam.

But she'd wait. The children had a game to win first, and they wouldn't be happy about the rest of the family getting stuck in a war zone.

———————◉———————

SHE GAVE THEM THE FIRST part of the news on their short walk from the schoolyard back home.

As she had predicted they were quite happy to hear it.

"I didn't want to go back in the first place," smiled Reenie, all lit up like a chandelier, and not for the first time, at the thought of remaining where they were. More like the hundredth. "But what about Papa?"

"And Henk and Kees?" Asked Billy, who worshipped his big brothers.

"And Rika?" Reenie inquired.

"Your *vader* and I are hoping they'll be coming to live here, too," Florentine told them, wording it carefully. "But you have to understand. It depends." She found she couldn't go on without crying and so stayed silent for a moment.

"On what?" Reenie asked her, putting an arm around her mother.

"On whether or not our country can get out from under the Germans," Florentine replied.

Chapter Three

1940 - 1941
Amsterdam, The Netherlands and Brooklyn, New York

INITIALLY, AND INCREDIBLY, once the *bezetting,* the occupation, began, most matters in Amsterdam seemed to go on as usual, or so it seemed to Rika, Henk and Kees.

At least, that was the way it transpired at first. Nazi red, white and black swastika flags started appearing all over town, of course, but that was to be expected, even though the Dutch hated to see those awful banners flying in place of their own red, white, and blue flag. German soldiers were seen on the streets, too. A lot of them came across as polite, even somewhat friendly. That wasn't what anyone expected.

The Queen began making radio broadcasts to the people at the end of May. "Do not despair," she urged her people. "Do everything that is possible for you to do in the country's best interest." She was attempting to guide them from afar and encourage everyone to resist the Nazi occupation.

On July 28th, which just happened to be Rika's fourteenth birthday, a new program, Radio Oranje, started broadcasting on the BBC station from London. "Radio Oranje here," the program always began, "the voice of the combatant Netherlands."

The first broadcast began with another address from the Queen. From then on, there would be news every night at nine o'clock, in Dutch. Real news, not the skewered kind the Nazis put on the airwaves, always rewritten in such a way to make themselves look as good as they possibly could.

"Radio Oranje. The Nazis will hate that," Kees grinned.

So did Rika. Yes, they surely would!

That was because orange was the Dutch royal family's color, from all the way back in 1544, when the lineage of the royal family began with a king called William of Orange. The Royal Family was from the House of Oranje-Nassau. In fact, "Oranje-Nassau" was even their last name.

"Oranje boven," a little saying that meant "orange on top," or "orange above all," which was a happy nod to the royals and the whole Dutch way of life, had always been popular. It was even the title of a song. After the invasion, the phrase became even more precious to the loyal Dutch people.

As far as colors went, their beloved orange had never seemed to be more important.

The Nazis figured that out, especially after some wonderfully gutsy people had scrawled graffiti reading "oranje boven" onto the walls in various locations. Incredibly, the Nazis even went so far as to *ban* the wearing or displaying of the color orange! They saw it as a sign of resistance. Which it was, of course, but what a thing to do, outlawing a color! No one was supposed to wear it or plant orange flowers or anything. Ridiculous!

Rika decided that when next winter came she had better not wear her favorite orange scarf out in public, insane as the idea of *not* flaunting it happened to be. Her world had started to turn upside-down.

Yet at the same time, the strange ban on the pleasant color was enough to give Rika a tiny spark of hope. If the Nazis felt they had to take such a measure, and were trying to kick orange out of the rainbow, of all the crazy ideas in all the world, they must have known, on some inner level, that they were already totally beaten in Holland. They couldn't outlaw what the people felt on the inside by banning a color on the outside, or take away everyone's love and respect for

the royal family. No, no way, they just couldn't legislate that. It was an
insane prospect, and nothing was ever that simple anyway.

Banning a color. Seriously, how ridiculous could they get?

It reminded her of the old Dutch saying, "They're making an
elephant out of a mosquito." That's what they were doing, those Nazis.

Oranje boven!

———— ◉ ————

FLORENTINE DIDN'T TELL anyone this, especially her two
children, but she longed to get another telegram from Julius.

She wished for one as she made the children their meals, as she
walked to the flower shop on Third Avenue in Bay Ridge, which was
two blocks up the street from her house, and as she arranged flowers in
vases for her customers to give as gifts. All day, every day. She lived to
hear more news of her family.

A few additional telegrams arrived, including a birthday telegram
that came for her in the beginning of December that same year, 1940.
Always the message was similarly cryptic, though that one added
"happy birthday." Nothing much else was said. "Doing well. Julius and
H K R." Henk, Kees and Rika.

Were they really doing all that well, living, as they were, under the
Nazis?

Of course, if they weren't, they couldn't say so in a telegram that
might have been intercepted. It was known, even in America, that the
Nazis read civilian mail, looking for spies or saboteurs or heaven only
knew what else.

Florentine had to wonder. What could be going on in Amsterdam?

———— ◉ ————

THE FIRST STRANGE MEASURE involving the Jews was that
Julius had to register the bookstore he owned as a "Jewish business."

That had happened right away in May 1940. For quite some time after that, though, that was it.

Julius Spranger sold his business, and the family's apartment, to his best friend, Bram Van Der Graaf. The plan was that the minute the Nazis were defeated he'd sell them right back to Julius.

Food rationing started right away for everybody, not just Jews. Even that really wasn't too terrible.

Just the same, the Dutch, including the Sprangers, who had always considered themselves 100% Dutch rather than specifically Jewish, were becoming uneasy.

The Jewish immigrants who had fled the measures enacted against them in Germany were even more so. Rika knew several of those transplanted German Jewish girls, like her buddies Liesel Hoffmeier and Susi Kleiner at school. Both of them came from Berlin. Their reports of the way they had been treated back in Deutschland sounded worthy of a horror movie, especially when they told her what they had witnessed firsthand on Kristallnacht, when the Nazis destroyed Jewish businesses and synagogues all over the country in retaliation for a Jewish boy's murder of a German diplomat.

But all good things always came to an end, and so it was with this lull.

After that, the Nazis began to show their true colors. They started instituting one measure after another against the Jewish population, all out of pure hate as sanctioned by Hitler.

It began slowly, similar to the way a coiled snake will remain coiled, watching its prey, right before it strikes.

Lying in wait.

On January 7, 1941, the situation worsened. It started on a small enough scale, or so it seemed, with a ban on allowing Jews to go to the movies.

Good old Bram Van Der Graaf, their father's best friend, who just happened to own a cinema, came to see the Sprangers right after the decree was issued. "None of you are to worry," he told them. "It's *my* movie theater. I don't care what those Germans say about who can enter it and who can't. I own it. The Nazis don't. You'll be allowed in, as always."

And they did continue to attend the movies for a little while longer, though not in the manner they once had, where they went in through the front door, choose their own seats, and ran back and forth to the refreshment stand Bram's wife, Charlotta, maintained, just as many times as they liked. Those days were over.

Instead, Bram would sneak them in through a back door to the theater, reachable through a courtyard located behind the building, with a narrow path leading from the street. He'd spirit them up the rear service staircase and lead them to the last private box on the right side of the tier of balcony seats.

No tickets were sold for that box. Ever. Bram saw to that, telling Betje Van Beek, his wife's friend who ran the ticket booth, that too many seats in that box needed to be repaired, when they actually didn't, and wartime was no time to start a renovation. He kept the box locked, except when he opened it for the Sprangers.

The siblings, often joined by their father, were lucky enough to still get in to see some films, but they hated having to sneak into this beloved theater. They missed walking right in with the same freedom as everybody else.

The Spranger kids knew better than to complain. Bram was risking getting into a lot of trouble by letting them inside his theater in the first place, though a lot of the usual joy of going to see a movie was out of it.

They also missed being able to greet Bram's wife, Charlotta, at the refreshment stand, although Bram usually had some treats already stashed for them to enjoy in their box. They always, before, had been able to officially bypass Charlotta's friend Betje, who was the ticket seller, and old Gerritt Jansen, the ticket-taker, since they had gotten in for free for years. Even so, they used to give a cheery wave hello to

Betje and Gerritt whenever they saw them, and they'd talk to Paolo, the usher and handyman from Spain, too. Paolo was almost the same age as age as Kees. He didn't go to school. He just worked. Rika loved his accent and the sight of his dark cinnamon brown eyes.

On February 3, 1941, it was declared that all the Jews had to register with the new regime. They were going to have to carry identity cards wherever they went, special ones, marked with big J's, to immediately reveal they were Jews to any official who demanded to see them.

Later that same month, yet another restriction was enacted. The special curfew for Jews began. They had to be inside their houses by eight o'clock at night and remain there until six o'clock the next morning. Violate curfew, get arrested.

The changes were incremental, but with each one, it got worse.

The Jews began to get fed up. That was only natural under the circumstances, but did it ever earn the ire of the Nazis! There was a clash on the street. A member of the Dutch Nazi Party, the NSB, was killed, and a policeman got injured.

That was all the Nazis needed. It gave them "an excuse" for severe retaliation.

At the end of February, *four hundred and twenty-five* Jewish men and boys were arrested as "punishment" for the dead Dutch Nazi and the wounded cop from the street melee. It didn't matter if the guys who were taken into custody were involved or not. They were all arrested anyway. The prisoners were shipped off to concentration camps in Germany.

The Dutch weren't happy with this, or with the rest of what was starting to happen to the Jews, either, so they staged a massive general strike as a protest.

It was phenomenal. People stayed home from work. Students didn't go to school. They brought the city of Amsterdam to a total standstill. What a sight!

City employees, teachers, factory workers, shop owners, dock workers, ferry pilots, medical staff members – they *all* gleefully protested the Nazis by not showing up to do their jobs! Even the public transportation system was stopped in its tracks.

The drivers of a few trams left the station anyway. Rika watched in awe as one of them was set upon by several protesters who turned it over on its side!

The tram, once righted, returned to the station.

The strike went on for three terrific days, driving the Nazis berserk. It spread from Amsterdam to a few other towns, and, at first, gave Rika and her family a lot of hope that the large-scale protest might just be enough to change things.

It didn't.

By the time the Nazis suppressed it with their trademark vicious violence, nine people were dead.

Fifty were injured.

And two hundred *more* were placed under arrest.

The eight o'clock at night to six o'clock in the morning military curfew was now extended to affect the entire population.

The persecutions of the Jews didn't stop. It went right on, with more measures being enacted against them.

May finally came, and with it, the first hint of springtime was in the air. The season of renewal had once been Rika's favorite, but not during that awful year, 1941. The viselike grip on the Jews just *continued*.

The latest indignity was that Jews were banned from public places. That meant parks, cafes, and most restaurants, except for the ones allowing Jews only, which had to be marked with a sign.

Why were the Nazis doing all this? In the scheme of life, Rika wondered, what harm could it do to let Jews go into *a park*?

By June, they were also prohibited from going to public swimming pools. Heaven forbid that a Jew could take a swim!

In September, worst of all, the Nazis would no longer let Jewish students attend state schools! They had to attend *alternate* educational establishments, ones for Jews only, where, presumably, they wouldn't "poison" the non-Jews with their presence. Or something.

Rika met up with Liesel Hoffmeier and Susi Kleiner on the first day at the new school that none of them really wanted to suffer the humiliation of having to attend. Liesel said with a sigh, "This situation here is getting to be like how we were treated in Berlin all over again."

Rika, who was becoming increasingly frightened with every new anti-Jewish rule, could only nod distractedly. This latest affront didn't look good to her, to put it mildly.

What kind of injustices would happen next?

At least her new school turned out to be a decent, congenial place. It was almost cozy, in spite of the times. The pupils and teachers were all Jewish, and every one of them was being subjected to the same list of indignities in the outside world. So the staff tried, to the best of their ability, to create as caring a community as possible for the students while they were within the walls of the school. There was a rare sense of togetherness and camaraderie there.

Even so, underlying everything at school, and elsewhere, was the increasing fear of the unknown. Their fate was not as secure now as it had been before the invasion, that was for sure. Most of them had never even thought of "their fate" until the Jew-hating Germans showed up.

There were constant rumors that all of the Jews were being earmarked for deportation. The teachers wanted to give their charges as many good days as possible while they were still all there, in Holland, and in this horrible mess together.

Rika felt a deep sense of foreboding.

———◦———

IN BROOKLYN, IN AMSTERDAM, and all over the world, people listened to their radios on December 7, 1941, in shock.

The Japanese had started another war on the other side of the world. Emperor Hirohito, and his Minister of War, General Tojo, were just as much on the march in Asia as Hitler was in Europe. They were in league with Hitler, and so were with the Italians, who also had a dictator running the show, one Benito Mussolini.

The Japanese made a vicious air attack on a U.S. naval bases located at Pearl Harbor on the Hawaiian Islands, which were under the auspices of the United States. This was done to cripple the American's Pacific Fleet.

After that, the United States, a country that had tried to remain neutral, declared war on Japan.

Once that happened, Hitler, Japan's vile ally, declared war on the United States.

The communications between Julius and Florentine stopped completely. There weren't any further telegrams. Rumor had it that the Nazis were now monitoring communications between the two countries, so Florentine figured that was why she no longer heard even the slightest word from home.

She had to wonder what those Nazis were doing now, though, employing people to steam open envelopes from America and read other people's private mail? They probably were.

Unbelievable!

Now Florentine could not know, from one day to the next, whether her husband and children were alive overseas or not.

Chapter Four

May and June 1942
Amsterdam, The Netherlands

———— ◉ ————

RIKA COULDN'T HELP but admire her wonderful father.

Julius had been trying his best to keep Henk, Kees and Rika on an even keel, or at least, as even a one as possible, in spite of everything. It had only partially worked. But he tried.

He'd told them to use the collection of restrictions on their free time to concentrate more heavily on their studies. If they couldn't go to parks, or swimming pools, or theaters, save for Bram's since he still snuck them in, they could use their abundance of free time to get higher grades.

All three of the children were smart but not particularly interested in becoming scholars. Even so, their dad got them to make more of an effort. There really wasn't much else to do anyway.

Julius had even found a way around some of the Nazi restrictions on his business. He went to the bookstore often because Bram's son Nikolaas, who was twenty-five, was now running it and had to be trained. Nikolaas even received a salary, but unofficially, it was still Julius's store.

He'd attempted to keep to his family's traditions whether the Nazis approved of them or not. They had never been particularly religious, but now, they kept the Sabbath candles lit on Friday nights. Mothers were supposed to be the ones to light them, so Papa asked Rika to stand in for her absent Mama. She was honored to comply.

They quietly celebrated each of the Jewish holidays, though not at the synagogue, just from inside of their apartment. There wasn't any raucous singing or spoken prayers, of course; everything even vaguely religious was whispered. The walls between their apartment and the ones on either side of it were thin. Though the neighbors remained friendly, if distant, it was hard, in those days, to know who was on their side and who wasn't.

The Amsterdam branch of the family couldn't help but wonder what was going on with the ones in America. How was Florentine faring? What about Verena and Willem? By 1942 the children were thirteen and twelve. Surely *they* weren't going to a segregated school or having to whisper their Sabbath prayers. They could mix with anybody and say their prayers outright.

Rika was beginning to think the whole idea of doing such things sounded almost like a miracle to her.

All of them believed that, while matters were bad, at least they weren't worse. They thought they could live with segregated schools, a business put in someone else's name, and no access to the public places where Jews were banned, so long as that was the end of it, and there wasn't anything else piled on top of what was already there.

Yet the rumors of deportations continued, frightening them all. There was talk of shipping the Jews off to work camps, where they could be put to "good use," at least from the Nazi perspective, assisting the German war effort. Never mind that helping the Nazis was the last thing the Jewish people had any desire to do so. Their opinion wouldn't count.

If the Nazis sent all the Jews away to work, where exactly would they be going? And what would they do once they got there?

It was May again, May 1942, and suddenly there was a new regulation.

This was the creepiest one yet.

All Jews had to wear six-pointed yellow stars on their clothing!

The stars had the word "Jood," Dutch for "Jew," printed on them. They were made of cloth, and the Jews had to not only wear them but *buy* them. They were also being forced to give up clothing ration tickets for them!

The stars had to be securely sewn onto their outerwear. Not pinned. Sewed. The Nazis probably thought that having to sew the stars would be more aggravating to the Jews because it would take longer.

It wasn't going to be possible to wear just any jacket or coat someone had on a cool day. They could only go out and about in one that had the star sewn onto it.

It would be even worse in the summer, on days when no jackets were needed, Rika thought miserably. They'd have to sew a star onto their dresses or shirts. Everyone only got four of them, so they would have to keep sewing a star onto one outfit, and removing it, in order to sew it the next day onto another.

On the day they purchased their awful stars, Kees called a family meeting in their apartment.

"We need to make a plan," he whispered to the others as they sat around the dining room table. "This is going too far. Now they're effectively branding us with these things." He picked up one of the stars that Rika had cut out of the cloth sheet of four and waved it around. "You know this is all going to get worse."

Henk nodded. "If we prance around in these stars, one look at us and everyone will know we're Jewish. There can't be a good reason for the *Duitsers* doing this." *"Duitsers"* was the Dutch word for Germans.

"It's probably to make it easier to identify us. And then *deport* us," Kees nodded. "They want us out of here. I hate them so much you can't even imagine it."

"Oh, I can," Rika said with feeling. She was ready to cry over the new star regulation. It was awful.

"There's rumors flying all over town," added Henk. "Petrus Prins told me."

Petrus Prins was the son of a man who had joined the Dutch Nazis, known as the NSB. The boy had been one of Henk's best friends, and despite his father's dictates against socializing with Jews, he had the courage to stay nominally in touch with his old friend Henk. "Petrus said that they're definitely going to send us all away to work camps in Germany, and put us to work helping with *their* war effort. It's the plan. All! And soon."

"How soon?" Rika gasped, but the others had no definite answer to that one.

"We need to do something," Kees went on. "We have to start by getting forged papers saying we're Christians. Different names, even. That will give us a chance to get out from under all of this." He gestured towards the star again, right after throwing it down on the table in disgust.

"I can do something about that," Julius said quietly. "I, ahem, know of *a way.*"

That was as far as he could tell them about it. His children knew not to ask any questions.

"I'll get right on this tomorrow," Julius promised them.

He had always been a man of his word, so his children did not doubt that he would succeed.

———————●———————

THE NEXT MORNING RIKA went to school as usual. She had to walk there now, and it was a hike. Jews were no longer allowed on public transportation.

She hated that walk, not because it was so long, although that, too. She couldn't stand it since she found it unbearable the way people suddenly looked at her with the yellow star so visible on her light pink spring coat.

Most of them looked at her with pity. Some shook their heads or clicked their tongues. Others made a special point to smile and nod hello, which she appreciated, yet it was only due to them feeling sorry for her. At least they were trying to be nice, but still.

A few others, though, shot her icy glares, loaded with hostility. Or they smirked. The Dutch may have been a mostly tolerant people, but they had their share of individuals who hated Jews, too.

Rika didn't like to be stared at either way. She felt like some kind of a branded freak.

Later that afternoon, when she got home, her father was there in the apartment, and he was smiling. That was a rare event.

"It's under control," he whispered, since the walls might have ears, without elaborating further. "You're not to worry. It may take a few weeks, but it's in the works." Right away Rika knew exactly what he meant.

He had a camera in hand and told her to stand by the wall so he could take her picture. Rika was happy to oblige. He told her it would be for her new identity card.

"Now take mine, Rika," he said, still whispering.

She did. Her father took the boys' photos when they returned home, and then, they thought, they'd be all set.

"We'll be moving," Julius told them with a wink. "To Naaldwijk, near the Hook of Holland."

The Hook of Holland was a seaport. Ships left from there. They probably wouldn't be able to board one, since it was wartime, Rika thought, but it sounded like a good plan to her anyway. They had a better chance of maybe getting on a ship if they lived near a port.

They'd probably sail off to some other country the very second the war ended and that became feasible, or maybe even sooner, so she smiled at the thought.

She hadn't had such an expression on her pretty face in so long that her smile muscles seemed rather stiff.

Oh, well. Perhaps soon, in Naaldwijk, she might be transformed back into the cheerful girl she once had been again.

Funny how a change of name, and the absence of a "J" on an identity card, could do that for you.

———————⟡———————

A THURSDAY AT THE BEGINNING of June was supposed to be *the day*.

Julius had told his children, on the Wednesday morning before they were to move, that they'd have to leave most of their stuff in the apartment. It wouldn't be a good idea to walk along the streets carrying luggage. Not when they were basically trying to escape from Amsterdam and did not want to attract attention to the fact.

Bram's son Nikolaas was going to be moving in after they left. He and Bram would find a way to get their clothes, and some of their other items, to them, a little while afterwards. Julius said if they could wear two layers of clothes rather than one, it might be a good idea. If that worked, they could each arrive in Naaldwijk with a second outfit.

"Go to school today as usual," he added. "Don't act like it's your last day there. Tell no one."

None of the children would. They knew better. Besides, students disappeared from school these days all the time. No one usually knew why, or where they went, whether it was to a new life with forged identities, like they were going to do, or into hiding, or if they'd been rounded up and sent away by the Germans already.

Rika had to wonder how her father had arranged for a new place to live in Naaldwijk. They knew nobody there, as far as she'd ever known anyway, but she trusted him completely.

All would work out. She was sure.

She was wrong.

———————⟡———————

WEDNESDAY NIGHT, RIKA couldn't wait to get home.

She had been distracted all day at school to the point that her history teacher had disciplined her twice, but no matter. She'd never see that woman again.

The young girl had been thinking about what she could sneak out of her room in her handbag. It was a large one, and could accommodate useful items, like her toothbrush and toothpaste, but also she could take some of her jewelry, and a few intricate pieces of her mother's that Florentine had left behind. She decided she could hide them in a cosmetic bag. Maybe it would be best to wrap them in a handkerchief first.

She wished she could take her orange scarf, or wear it, but that one was warm and heavy and could have only been considered appropriate attire in the depths of a Netherlands winter. Or at least, it could have been worn on a cold day before the Nazis decreed the color was an act of resistance. Not now. Even so, it would have been wonderful to walk away from Amsterdam in the official color of the Dutch royal family.

Once she got home to the apartment she found it was deadly quiet. Ominous, somehow.

It gave her a sense of uneasiness.

The boys hadn't returned home from school yet. Her father was nowhere to be found, either. Chances were, he was still out, wherever he had to go, to meet his contact and pick up their new identity cards.

Rika wondered what her new name was going to be and how long she'd have to be using it. She didn't care *what* she'd have to call herself in order to put one over on the Nazis.

She told herself she was bright enough to get used to anything in order to get through this war. So was her father, and so were Henk and Kees.

The boys came home shortly after Rika arrived, but there was no sign yet of their father.

Rika started to cook dinner. There was no reason not to have a hearty meal on their last night at home, she thought. They couldn't take any of the perishable food with them. She made omelets with cheese.

The clock in the kitchen seemed to tick more loudly than usual as she cooked.

Where was her father?

Should they be worried?

"I don't like this," Henk said as they sat down to eat without Julius. "It's not like Father to stay out this late. It's less than an hour until curfew."

Curfew was at eight of clock. Surely Julius would arrive home by then.

Except he didn't.

He was also a no show at nine, ten or eleven o'clock that night.

The three siblings were still up. Still anxious.

Waiting. And waiting some more.

They remained wide awake, increasingly concerned while hoping to see a father who, they feared, simply wasn't coming home.

This wasn't at all like Julius Spranger. Something must have happened.

Finally Kees said uncertainly, "Look, he probably was out too late to get home and stayed with friends for the night." He did not sound like he really believed that, though.

People, especially Jewish people, did that a lot so they wouldn't be caught out past the curfew. Perhaps Julius had stayed put, wherever he was, however he could, and would be home in the morning.

But their father had never done that before.

Ever.

———— ◉ ————

RIKA HAD FINALLY FALLEN asleep sitting up on the sofa.

She awoke the next morning shortly after seven, according to the watch she was still wearing, when there was a knock on the door.

"It's me, Bram," she could hear her father's best friend saying out in the hallway.

"Bram!" Rika leapt up, made her way to the door, and let him in.

The boys had long since retired to their room. They emerged at that point.

"Where's Papa?" Rika asked him.

Kees shook his head. "Not here."

"Oh," Rika replied, deflated.

Henk asked Bram, "Would you happen to know where he is, Bram?"

"Let's sit down for a quick minute, shall we?" Bram replied.

Which wasn't a reply at all, but an evasion.

Rika felt her heart constrict.

Something was definitely wrong here.

The boys and Bram settled themselves at the dining room table. Rika busied herself by putting on the kettle to make what passed for wartime coffee. She wished she was anywhere else, about to hear some different kind of news, rather than whatever was coming.

"I'm sorry to have to tell you this," Bram began at last, as Rika sat down and joined the others. "Your father made a contact through the bookstore. A member of the Resistance, or so he thought. Name's Joep Alderink. He claimed to be making forged identity papers for all of you."

Kees seized on the word. *"Claimed?"*

Bram nodded wearily. "Claimed. Falsely. He took a lot of money from your father, who was waiting behind his bookstore last night, where he thought he was safe, to meet up with Alderink. Thank goodness he arranged to meet that *bastaard* outside, at least. My son Nikolaas was there too, of course, running the store for your dad, and if Julius had set up an indoor meeting, Nikolaas would have been in trouble, too. In any event, my son saw and heard everything. Alderink showed up. He brought along a member of the Gestapo, and they arrested your father on the spot."

"Arrested?" Rika exclaimed. *"No!"* It came out as a wail.

"Yes. I'm so sorry to tell you this. Nikolaas claimed no knowledge of your father or what he was doing outside when he got questioned, and the damned Gestapo believed him. They were interested in taking your father, not Nik. My son thinks Alderink was working undercover for them. Unfortunately they're probably going to be sending Julius away to a work camp, and that's if he's lucky. A prison if he isn't." Bram didn't add that with these Nazi crazies, execution was even a possibility.

"This is a catastrophe," Rika murmured as Bram went on.

"The authorities might also be sending someone over here to pick all of *you* up, since the order for the false identity cards included one for each of you, too, so I suggest we down this coffee as fast as possible and you come away with me. Right now, immediately, and without any hesitation. I'm sorry if I sound like I'm giving orders here, but I think this situation warrants it. You're going into hiding and you're going in *today*. Drink up fast and get dressed, children."

Normally her brothers would have bristled at being called "children," they were too old for that, but they didn't squawk about it this time. All three Sprangers did as they were asked. The coffee scalded Rika's tongue on the way down her throat, but she was so upset and frightened that she almost didn't notice.

Father in a jail or on the way to a work camp! There were such terrible rumors circulating about those camps. The hundreds of men who had been taken to a camp after that street fight back in 1941, when the Dutch Nazi got killed and the police officer was wounded, were all sent to a camp called Mathausen.

They never came back.

Bram didn't have to ask her twice to move quickly. She got dressed and put her shoes on in less than a minute.

Once they were ready and back in the front room, Bram gave them another command. "Take those stars off your coats, right now. You're not going on the street dressed like that."

Rika picked up the sewing scissors that they now kept near the door so that it would be handy when they needed to cut one of the stars loose. She got it off her jacket with a few deft snaps of the scissors, then handed it to Kees. He removed his star and gave the scissors to Henk for the same purpose.

Soon all three were mercifully starless.

"Give me your identification cards, too," Bram added. "I'll make sure to burn them later. You can't be carrying cards with J's on them if, heaven forbid, you're ever caught."

"And boys, put some hats on so you won't stand out too much on the street with that dark hair," Bram added. "It marks you as Jewish." He glanced at Rika and told her, "With that dark blonde hair of yours, at least you don't have to wear one."

"No, but I want to," Rika told him. She pulled her favorite hat off the hat rack. Her mother had bought it for her right before leaving for America. It was a little white hat with a short brim and had blue ribbon around it. She loved it, and wherever they were headed, she wanted something from her mother to take along.

That was when she remembered something else. The jewelry in her mother's dresser drawer. She had forgotten to retrieve it the night before in all the confusion about Julius not arriving home.

"Let me just grab something," she said, though she meant several other somethings, and quickly fled the room, to Bram's consternation, running straight to her parents' bedroom. It only took her a moment to scoop up several pieces of the jewelry and stuff it into her purse. She didn't wait to find a cosmetic bag to hide it in, either, just threw it all straight inside the handbag.

"Let's go!" Bram was almost shouting.

Rika scurried like a little rat back to the front room and out the door of the apartment.

She had never seen Bram look so discomposed. His florid face was almost turning purple as he led them, calmly, along their street, and around a few familiar corners.

Halfway there, Rika recognized the route. Bram was taking them to his theater.

Chapter Five

June 1942
Amsterdam, The Netherlands

THEY ENTERED THE THEATER through the path to the courtyard, as they usually when Bram was sneaking them in, and went in the through back entrance once again. Bram opened the rear door with a heavy-looking key.

Strange as it was to have such a thought at the time, Rika had almost hoped they'd walk in the *front* door, since the stars were no longer sewn onto their coats, after all.

Oh, well. It would have been nice not to feel like they were outlaws, slithering in.

It still wasn't even eight o'clock in the morning yet. "We don't open for hours," Bram said, "so there should be no problem with concealing the three of you right now." Once they were inside, he locked the back door behind them and finally started to look as kind and relaxed as he normally did. The man must have been terrified to have just ferried three Jewish kids outside on the street that morning.

"Here's what I'm thinking," he finally said. "This is a movie house now, but years ago, it was a live action theater. There's a dressing room backstage, on the first level, that hasn't been used in about two decades. Boys, that's where you're going. There used to be two of them, but I converted one into my office. It's right next door to yours. Rika, I'm putting you upstairs, in a storeroom we don't use that's right across the hallway from the projection booth room." He added, "Both of these rooms are always kept locked, so no one on my staff will ever think twice about them remaining that way."

Henk looked at Kees first and Rika second before turning to Bram. "Why does Rika have to go to whole a different room?" He asked. "She should be staying with us."

"Yes," agreed Kees, "she should."

"That wouldn't be a good idea," Bram explained. "How shall I phrase this? These rooms where you'll be hiding aren't exactly luxury suites. Do you know what I'm saying?"

All three of the Sprangers gave him a puzzled look.

"There's no water closet in either one," Bram elaborated. "No toilet, in other words. You'll have to use chamber pots. I'll get them for you, but I really don't think your sister should be staying in the same room as you boys are when you're doing what people have to do, if you know what I mean."

At that point, they got it.

Bram took the trio over to the old actor's dressing room in the theater's backstage area first. It was a long rectangular room with dressing tables along one wall. They had light-up mirrors that still worked, but those, Bram said, were not to be turned on, ever. "I've got blackout curtains on the window over there," he added, pointing to a large rectangular window covered with pleated black cloth. "You have to be extremely careful in here. Remember, there's a nice courtyard out there, with flowers and even some benches. Ten buildings are surrounding this one. You can't talk loudly. Ever. There's always the possibility that someone could be standing right outside."

Bram added that he would be bringing in some bedrolls later that morning for them to sleep on. He'd also supply flashlights, batteries, and plenty of books for all three of them to read so that they would have something to do all day. He'd be bringing them food to eat, too.

"Now why don't I show you the way upstairs so you can see where I'm stashing Rika?" He added.

They crossed from the backstage area, went through the auditorium, and into front the lobby area. From there they proceeded up the stairs to the balcony level and box seats, and on, still further, up an additional, extremely narrow staircase behind an inconspicuous door. It led up a steep flight of steps to the floor where the projection room was located at the top of the theater. Bram flicked a light switch on as they entered the hallway.

There were two well-used storerooms flanking the projection room that held old equipment and metal film canisters. "Those we use," Bram explained, "but this one, we don't." He opened a door right across the hallway from the projection room.

It was a small room, and it smelled musty, as if it hadn't been aired out in at least a decade, but Rika figured she'd take it any way she could get it. "I realize it isn't much," Bram began apologetically.

Rika interrupted him. "No, it's fine, Bram, really."

"It's not too much larger than the size of your bedroll will be," he went on, "but I'll get you whatever you need. A chamber pot, a bedroll with some good blankets, books. It locks from the inside, and after my wife or I come to see you, you have to lock it once we leave. But you must be even more careful up here than the boys need to be, Rika. There are two projectionists. They could be in the hallway at any time, smoking cigarettes, or going downstairs to the lounge for a quick break once the movie is started. They go all over the place. You'll need to keep the light off while they're working, though you can use a flashlight to read if you put a blanket over your head and face the wall opposite the door. You can't let any light slip out from under that doorway or they'll know something is up. I do trust them both, but they are not to know you're here, and you can't afford to give them a clue. I'll come to you with food, and so will my wife, Charlotta. My daughter knows nothing about all this, and I want to keep it that way, so she won't be visiting you, but my son Nikolaas might."

Rika remembered that Bram's daughter Emmi had been best friends with her little sister Verena.

That made her wonder where Verena was right now. Probably in school in New York, or riding a swing in a playground. Maybe their brother Willem was pushing her on the swing, and they were running around, laughing, free. It was such a pleasant thought to have, especially as she looked at the small, dreary room.

"It's going to take me a little time to get everything together," Bram added. "I can go home and will bring back the chamber pots and bedrolls before the staff starts to show up. Meanwhile, there's that pile of old tarpaulins there, in the corner. For now, why don't you pull those out and sit on them?"

Rika replied, "That sounds good." She was exhausted from the ordeals of the past two days, and the tarps looked like they'd be perfectly fine for her to lie down on and take a nap.

"All three of you," Bram said sternly, turning to include the boys, "will need to move around as little as possible during the hours when the theater is operational. Try to make absolutely no sounds. None. When the movies are on, the soundtrack should cover any noises you might make, but when there's silence between the shows, or before and after they start, and while the staff is still here, don't even move if you can help it. There are people all over this place, whenever this theater is open for business, and that's every day of the week, so you've got to be exceptionally quiet when they're here. If there's ever an emergency, and *only* if it's vital, you can go into my office and call me at home, but *only* after the place is closed for the night."

"We know the number," Kees nodded.

Bram said, "Good. Now on to another subject. Once the masses go home at closing time, wait for an hour, and after that, you three are free to roam around. You can visit one another. Walk back and forth to get some exercise. Raid the refreshment stand, even. Charlotta runs it so she won't raise an alarm if any of the goodies are missing. You can even wash up in the restrooms. Just be careful once the place is open every day."

The three teens nodded. They had no intention of not being compliant.

Their well-being depended on it.

———————◦——————

BRAM SAID HE WAS GOING to bring the boys back to their quarters and go home to get supplies. He explained to Rika, "Like I was saying, you have to lock the door from the inside with the sliding bolt chain as soon as I leave."

"All right," Rika replied, and after Bram and the boys exited, she did.

The overhead light was still on.

"Douse the light, Rika. I can see it blazing below the door. That won't do."

Rika dutifully turned it off.

"Oh," she breathed.

She'd never known a blackness quite like this before. The room didn't have a window like her brothers' did. Not a single speck of light managed to make its way in.

"I'll be back soon," Bram promised. "I'll knock twice. You'll know when the projectionist arrives because he'll turn the hallway light on, and you'll be able to see that through the bottom of the door. For now I'm going to turn it off, okay? Oh, and don't forget you can visit the boys a whole lot later, after the last show tonight."

"*Ja,*" Rika agreed as pleasantly as she could under such extraordinary circumstances.

After the *last* show? It wasn't even time for the *first* show yet.

Rika wished Bram had left the hallway light on.

She heard the others walking away, clomping down the steep wooden stairs, probably trying to do so quietly but not really succeeding.

How had all of this happened?

Yesterday she was attending what she thought was to be her last day of school before moving with her father and brothers to a new town with a new identity and a new name.

Now here she was, a girl with a father who had been arrested, no home either here or there, living in a pitch-dark room, and with nothing more than the clothes on her back and the contents of her purse.

The Nazis. That was how it had happened. The important thing now was to be glad she was, at least, safe, for the moment anyway, and to get herself through this.

Rika felt around until she came to the pile-up of tarpaulins. She took off her coat and removed her precious little hat, the one from her mother. At least she still had that. She put them on the tarpaulin pile beside her. Remembering she had grabbed some of her mother's jewelry, too, and how she had thrown a handful of it willy-nilly into her handbag, she decided she could sort that out some night after the projectionists left. It wouldn't do to try and do that while one of them was there, or now, in the dark. Jewelry was made of metal and the pieces might clink together.

The idea almost was enough to make her laugh, though she didn't dare. What would a projectionist think if he heard *clinking noises* coming out of the unused storeroom?

The answer to that wasn't funny, though. If either one of those guys ever heard it, they'd know the room was definitely being utilized now.

That could be dangerous.

RIKA LAY PROPPED AGAINST the part of the tarpaulin that wasn't hosting her coat, hat, and purse. What to do in the dark except nod off for a little while? She was so tired. Everything that had been on the way to going right had, instead, gone so crazy, and happened so fast.

Where had her father been taken? She was concerned for him in addition to all the rest of it.

They hadn't had breakfast that morning, just the fake coffee, and she was very hungry, but there was nothing to be done for that at the moment, either.

It wasn't more than five minutes before Rika had drifted into a welcome though fitful sleep.

———— ◉ ————

TRUE TO HIS WORD, BRAM came back within about two hours. Rika awoke the second or third time when she heard the two soft knocks coming onto the door of her hiding place.

"Rika! Come on, open up," Bram was saying on the other side of the locked door. "Open the latch."

She could make out where it was from the dim light coming in from the hallway. Bram must have turned the light on.

She got the inside latch open.

"There you are," Bram said to her with a smile. "And look who else is here to say hello."

His wife Charlotta came into the tiny room beside him. "Sweet girl, it's always nice to see you, although I wish it wasn't under circumstances like this." Charlotta reached out and hugged her. The girl was trembling.

"That's okay," Rika whispered. "You're both terrific to help my brothers and me like this."

"You Sprangers are like family," Charlotta assured her. She handed her a basket. "Bread and jam, a bottle of water and some apple fritters leftover from yesterday." She admitted sheepishly, "It's the best I could do on short notice. These should hold you for the rest of today, at least, and I promise, tomorrow the food will be better."

"Sounds fine to me," Rika assured her. "Don't feel like you have to fuss, Charlotta."

"What kind of a good hostess would I be if I didn't?" Charlotta replied, with a teasing smile on the outside, though all the while her heart was breaking on the inside at the whole necessity of having to leave this poor girl alone in such a musty room. That it had come to this!

Bram was holding some rolled-up bedding in one hand and a large shopping bag in the other. It held a flashlight, batteries, a chamber pot with a lid, and a few novels. "Here's some goodies so you can make yourself more at home in here," he told her. "Again, if you want to read with the flashlight, you have to put one of these blankets I've brought you over your head, so the projectionists don't see any light coming from in here under the door. You can leave the overhead light on for only about another half hour before the projectionist gets here and then you have to shut it off. *Have to*. His name's Bartol Kuijper. The other one is Gustav De Boon. Bartol's here during the weekdays, Gustav on the weekends." He winked. "But you're not to pop out of here and introduce yourself to either one of them."

"You know I won't," Rika said with a weak grin.

"Of course we know you won't," Charlotta assured her, reaching out a kind hand to squeeze the sweet girl's shoulder. "We know this arrangement isn't ideal, Rika. It's far from it. For the moment, though, we think it can work. We're going to try and find a better place for you and your brothers. In the meantime, just try your best to adapt."

"Nikolaas is staying in your apartment," Bram added, "since, as you know, I bought it from your father some time back, so that it would be in my hands for safekeeping. You'll get it back from us after the war, don't worry. My son's going to get a few of your dresses and nightgowns. Underwear, socks. Toothbrush, toothpaste, soap, good stuff like that. Is there anything else you'll need?"

Just about everything I left behind, Rika thought to herself. But she said, "Whatever he can get me will be fine."

"Now step out of there for a minute," Bram went on, "and let me spread those tarps across the floor. Keep your shoes off at all times, okay? The tarps can help muffle any sounds you might make if you get up and walk around in here."

There isn't much chance of that, Rika thought. It wasn't a spacious room. She'd probably only be getting up to use the chamber pot, and even at that, only when the movie was on and the sound of it could cover her moves.

Once the tarp had been spread out, this fine couple who were risking their lives for her said it was time they took their leave.

"We'll see you again tomorrow morning," Charlotta told her. "Courage, my dear!"

"Oh, she has plenty of that, Charlotta," Bram smiled. "Can't you tell? Just remember, Rika, watch for when the hallway light comes on under the door. That will mean Bartol is here. And turn off your overhead light."

With that, they left. They also switched off the light in the hall as they went on their way, and what little bit of brightness could have shone under the door was fully extinguished, as a result.

Rika turned her light off. Blackness again, worse than midnight.

She didn't know what to think about all of this. She *hated* the idea of Nikolaas going through her bureau drawers and picking out underwear, just *hated* it. He was a good-looking twenty-four-year-old guy, and she had always liked him, even had a bit of a crush on him, but this was so embarrassing. Ideally Charlotta should have been the one to go to the apartment and get her things.

"Ideally" had flown out the window.

Ha. What window? She didn't even have one here.

She wondered about what Charlotta had said. Would they really find a better location where she and her brothers could hide? Would it turn out to be better or even worse?

At least for now she was safe.

Rika sighed. She felt around for where Charlotta had placed the basket of food on the floor and took an apple fritter out of it to munch on. About all she could do in the dark at the moment was eat.

———◉———

ABOUT HALF AN HOUR of sitting in the dark later, Rika saw the dim glow of the hallway light, visible at the bottom of her door, come on.

Someone was whistling his way up the steps. Bartol?

It must have been.

That meant the theater would be filling up with customers soon.

Rika felt so scared. The projectionist booth was on the third floor of the theater and the last rows of balcony seats were underneath it.

What if she moved?

How sturdy was the floor beneath the tarpaulin?

Might it squeak?

And would anyone seated in the rear of the balcony below notice and think it was strange?

Don't be silly, she scolded herself. Everyone who came to the theater certainly knew somebody had to be on the third floor in order to run the movie. Even if they did hear anything coming from this floor, they would assume it was made by the projectionist, if they thought about it at all.

But what if there were Nazis in the audience, and they heard it, and then thought twice about it?

They might. They really and truly just might.

It was a legitimate concern.

Rika did not dare to move. How in the world was she going to do this, she wondered, day after day after day?

People were entering the theater. She could hear them, though the sound was a bit muffled, chattering as they seated themselves in the audience. It went on for what seemed like forever.

Rika needed to use the chamber pot, but was afraid to lift the lid, and do what had to be done over it, in the pitch-black dark.

About forty-five uncomfortable minutes later the movie finally began with the newsreel. It sounded like pure Nazi propaganda.

That was the bad news.

The good?

The volume was wonderfully loud. It came through the walls of her hideaway loud and clear. She could hear every single word.

That meant she could move, even use the chamber pot, and just in time, too.

It was also possible to listen to all of the newsreels and movies, and enjoy the plots, even if she couldn't see the films. She could *hear* them. Rika had always loved the movies. A comedy came on after the newsreel.

This, Rika finally smiled to herself, isn't going to be such a bad place to hide after all.

Chapter Six

June and July 1942
Amsterdam, The Netherlands

CHARLOTTA CAME BACK the next morning, knocking twice on the door.

Rika was more relieved to see her than she would ever admit. She was so happy to flick on the light switch and let the good woman in.

It had been a long previous first day and night in hiding. She hadn't ventured out of the room to roam around the theater yet, and the boys hadn't come up to visit her, either.

In addition, alone with her thoughts, she had been absolutely plagued with worries about her father, Julius.

Was he really all right?

Alive, still?

Or shot for trying to ensure their freedom with false identity cards?

If he was still among the living, where were the Nazis planning to send him?

And who had been this traitor, this Joep Alderink, who pretended to be a trusted contact and could provide Papa with the new identity cards? He must have either been a Nazi himself, or else he was working for them, and had turned her decent dad in.

Where had her father found him?

Was the creep really a forger, or at least, some kind of an artist, someone actually capable of creating false documents?

If so, who had pointed her father in his direction?

Or was he a total undercover fraud, trying to lure desperate Jews into a trap? He had, after all, turned their poor father right in to the Gestapo.

It kept Rika awake and in a state of anxiety, turning those thoughts over and over in her head, for almost the entire night. She only drifted off to sleep right before Charlotta's two knocks on the door pulled her back from an uneasy dream that had swastikas in it.

Rika switched on the light, opened the door, and said, *"Goedemorgen,"* greeting Charlotta with a forced cheerfulness that she didn't feel for one second. However, it was important, Rika thought, to be as polite as possible to the people who were hiding her. The Van Der Graafs were going above and beyond the call of duty.

"Hallo! Here you go," Charlotta smiled, first handing over a large canvas duffel bag. She looked so blonde and kind in the dim overhead light of the hiding place, almost like an angel. "Here's some goodies for you. Nikolaas picked out these two extra dresses for you, and this pair of pajamas. Underwear too. Socks. A bar of soap. I figure you'll need feminine products, but I can get you those." Charlotta laughed. "I didn't want to ask *Nikolaas* to try and arrange them for you. Who knows what he might have chosen?"

Rika smiled with relief at that as she reached for the duffel bag. "I will need some of those, yes, thanks." How embarrassing it would have been if *Nikolaas* had had to find them! It would be a couple of weeks yet before Rika would need any feminine supplies, but where those were concerned, it was always better to be prepared.

"Also, Bram asked me to tell you to keep everything you've got here in this duffel bag," Charlotta went on. "Everything. Always. All of your stuff. The dresses, the pajamas, and he even thinks you should put your purse, hat, and shoes in there. It's big enough. When you take off your dress at night, or change your socks, stash them in the bag. Fold the garments up as small as you can and keep them there. That way, if you ever have to leave here quickly, you can just pick up the one bag and go."

"That sounds like a good idea," Rika replied. "Yes." She didn't add how much the whole concept of having to dash away from this theater already scared her. Staying here might not have been too pleasant, but leaving didn't sound like a good option, either.

"When the clothes get dirty after a few weeks, you can give them to me, and I can wash them for you and bring them back. I've got two more of your dresses and another pair of pajamas that Nikolaas grabbed at home. We're keeping them for you. Spares, so you can switch off, as needed."

"Thank you," Rika said wholeheartedly. "For everything, Charlotta."

"Oh, it's no bother. And here's breakfast, lunch and dinner, along with some snacks." Charlotta handed over the bag that was in her other hand. "Sandwiches, mostly. They won't go bad. Some fruit, too, two hardboiled eggs, and a bottle of soda. Guess what kind?"

Rika shrugged, not having any idea.

"Oranje Benno. Orange soda. It's more popular than ever these days. Ha, I wonder why?" Charlotta joked.

"I think I can figure it out," Rika grinned.

Orange soda! It was amazing the Nazis hadn't banned it yet. Maybe they hadn't realized it existed. They probably would, and if they did, they'd ban it.

"Did you get out of here last night?" Charlotta finally asked.

"No, I...wasn't up for that," Rika replied. "Not last night."

"*Naturlich*. Tough day for you yesterday. Tonight, then. You shouldn't stay in here all cooped up all day and all night and not walk around the theater at least for a little bit, once everybody goes home."

That was easier for Charlotta to say, Rika thought. She wasn't the one who was all alone in the dark in here. Any little, tiny noise she had heard during the previous night had been enough to make her jump, even though mostly they were the harmless sounds of the building settling, or ones that could be heard from out in the street. Yet she said, "I will."

"Courage!" Charlotta smiled.

And unfortunately that was it. Charlotta went away again, and the long day stretched ahead of Rika.

While she still had some time before Bartol the projectionist arrived, Rika kept the light on and looked through the duffel bag. Nikolaas had chosen two summer dresses for her, a pair of pajamas with pants, and had even included a surprise. There, in an inner pocket of the bag, she found a photo of her mother, brother Willem and sister Verena. They were standing in front of their flower shop in Brooklyn. It had been sent to her before the Japanese attacked Pearl Harbor, before America entered the war, and before the communications between the USA to Holland stopped.

Rika was so happy to have it and to see the fresh smiling faces of the rest of her family that she almost cried.

One day, Rika vowed, I'll be there too.

She just didn't know when it might be, and dared not to let herself be reminded that a great big "if" was involved in the whole concept, too.

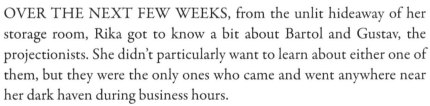

OVER THE NEXT FEW WEEKS, from the unlit hideaway of her storage room, Rika got to know a bit about Bartol and Gustav, the projectionists. She didn't particularly want to learn about either one of them, but they were the only ones who came and went anywhere near her dark haven during business hours.

Bartol was the happier guy of the two. She knew when he was coming up the stairs even before he switched the hallway light on because he was always whistling a jaunty song. He went sauntering, or so she imagined, into the projection room, and for the most part, stayed there, watching the movies, and waiting for the moment when he had to change from one reel on the projector to the other. Long movies weren't able to be shown with just one reel of film. He usually didn't leave the room except to go downstairs, probably to the refreshment stand or the men's room.

Gustav De Boon was a whole other matter.

He was only there on the weekend days, thank goodness, because sight unseen, he made Rika nervous.

Gustav bounded up the stairs, probably two at a time, sounding like a mad rhino on the charge. It scared her to death every time she heard it, even though she knew it was coming. After that, he would go into the projection booth, start the newsreel, wait for it to end, put on the first reel of the movie, and then he was out of there again, stampeding down the stairs before coming back up again several minutes later.

This went on three or four times during every movie.

He also liked to periodically pace around their floor. Gustav De Boon was a man who couldn't remain still if his life depended on it. She had to wonder what he would have done if he had to be stuck in *here.*

Before the first weekend was out, she even heard him sneaking a girl upstairs to watch the movie, right alongside of him in the booth.

As if it wasn't scary enough to have these two strangers, these projectionists, going back and forth near her hiding place every day, now there was this girl, too. She heard Gustav calling her "Marijke."

Rika could not see her and didn't want to. She didn't like her sharp, grating tone of voice.

The only good aspect of those Marijke visits, which Rika noticed seemed to happen every Sunday, was that Gustav usually stayed in the booth with her during the movie rather than running around the theater. The two lovebirds were only outside in the hallway or flying up and down the stairs when one showing ended and before the next one began.

Rika could sometimes feel just free enough to put her blanket over her head, face the far wall of her hideaway, turn on the flashlight, and read until the film was over.

That didn't always work because the storage room where she hid was too stuffy and hot. The room didn't come along with a fan. There wasn't a window for decent ventilation, either. Outside, when her hiding ordeal began, it was June, with summer approaching. The heat in the room seemed to increase every day, and that didn't go so well with the practice of Rika sticking her head under a blanket.

She was also afraid to sleep too much during the daytime because sleeping was too far beyond her control. What if she started to snore, or had a bad dream, and proceeded to cry out in her sleep? What if Bartol or Gustav or this Marijke gal *heard* her? It could morph into a disaster. Yet another one. The last thing she needed was for an additional calamity to befall her.

It was better to try and stay awake as much as possible while the others were there. She either listened to the movies or, if the current film wasn't one she particularly cared for, thought up stories in her head to entertain herself. She tried to remain alert. In a dark room with nothing better to do, though, that just didn't always work.

One thought she kept in mind, over and over again, every day, in fact, was that she had to think of herself as a tulip bulb.

It might have seemed like an odd choice to anybody else who wasn't in this situation, but in this one, it fit.

Tulip bulbs were planted under the ground, and that's exactly where she felt like she was, in this room that was usually so dark. Rika was underground.

Or very close to it.

She remembered the time her grandfather, Opa, her mother's wonderful father, the one whose death led to Mama, Verena and Willem's never-ending trip to America, had come to visit. Opa had a flower shop that Rika had never seen, back there in Brooklyn. She may have been only about five or six when her grandpa came over on an ocean liner to spend a month with them, but he had told her all about tulips, the Dutch national flower, and how lovely, and even almost magical, they were.

"A tulip begins with a bulb," she remembered him telling her. "It has to be planted down in the ground, twice as deeply as the height of the bulb. Nice and deep. That's where it stays for some time, and it makes roots. It remains there all through the wintertime. Then there's a metamorphosis of sorts. Still underground, the leaves start to grow. They push upwards through the earth until they break through the ground and rise right up out of the dirt. And then, do you know what happens, Rika? Then, they bloom. Where once there was a bulb in the dark, suddenly there will be a lovely, vivid, colorful flower."

It might happen for me, if I survive this war, Rika thought. I'm deep in the dark right now, that's for sure. But one day, if I'm lucky, I'll rise up and out of this, and I'll get my chance to bloom, too.

It was a story she kept telling herself.

She'd always end it by thinking, "Courage!"

———○———

ONE EVENING SHE HEARD Gustav and Marijke talking right outside of her door before the movie started. It sounded like they were sitting on the floor, drinking alcohol from a bottle.

"You better give me a sip!" Marijke demanded. It sounded like she was giving Gustav an imperial command.

"Me first," Gustav insisted.

"Then me second!"

This is all we need, Rika thought, rolling her eyes. They'll be drunk next. She felt those two were enough trouble when they were sober, bounding all over the building, and now they might be getting *drunk*.

She heaved a sigh of relief when they went back into the projection room, and soon, the newsreel began the next showing.

Chapter Seven

July through October 1942
Amsterdam, The Netherlands

———◦———

LIFE SEEMED TO BEGIN for Rika whenever the theater emptied out for the night and everyone, audience members and staff alike, went home. The three siblings considered the hiding place was their prison by day, their playground by night.

She could walk freely around the theater, go downstairs to the mezzanine level or the first floor, use the ladies lounge, have a sponge bath there or wash her hair in the sink, and even visit the refreshment counter and take whatever she wanted.

Henk and Kees would emerge from their backstage dressing room. It was so fortunate that theaters weren't built with too many windows since the movies had to be shown in the dark. No windows at all had been built into the auditorium. Sometimes the boys liked to navigate their way through the place, go upstairs and visit with Rika.

Henk and Kees had found two useful games in the old dressing room where they hid. There was a full deck of cards and a board game. Most of the time they came up and played cards in her room, all three sitting cross-legged on the floor. Some nights they brought her down to the dressing room, or they would sit in the theater seats and just talk, always keeping their voices low as a precaution, in spite of the fact that no one else was there. Who knew if anyone might be on the other side of the exit doors?

"It's certainly an unusual existence we have here," she said to them one night, and they all had a good laugh at the absurdity of it.

MATTERS IN THE OUTSIDE world worsened yet again in July. In fact, it was possible to believe they even seemed to increase on the square.

The Nazis sent out summonses to *hundreds and hundreds* of Jews, decreeing they were to report for "labor duty" in Germany.

The list of labor prospects was outrageous. It even included a whole lot of teenagers.

According to Charlotta, who heard it from Nikolaas, one of those summonses had arrived at the Spranger's old apartment *for Kees!*

At that point, Rika, Henk, and most especially Kees were more grateful than ever that the Van Der Graafs were hiding them. If they had remained at home the Nazis might have found Kees there and forced him to go away.

"This is not a good time for moving you three to another location," Bram told them one summer morning, in his office, hours before his staff had arrived. "You're safe here. The Nazis are going berserk out there, even blocking off streets and checking identity cards to round up Jews, and others, too. Some days they'll take anybody. I was hoping to move you to more comfortable hiding places, but for now, you've got to stay put."

"All's well here," Kees assured him.

"It's better than being cooped up someplace where we can't even move around at night," Henk added.

Rika didn't say anything, just nodded. The boys were hidden in a bigger and more comfortable room than she was. She had been looking forward to going elsewhere, although maybe remaining here wasn't exactly the worst idea in a world that contained Nazis on the hunt for Jews.

"I'm trying to get you new IDs," Bram continued. "It may take some time. Perhaps later this year you can be moved."

"Be careful," Rika breathed. When her father had gone for new IDs it had led to his arrest.

Something about the whole latest "labor duty" episode seemed to be "off," Charlotta told Rika on another day, and as a result, people were beginning to realize that. It was one thing to want to send the adults away to work in Germany for the war effort, but why would the Nazis want to put young teens to work? How much good could a bunch of kids do for them? They weren't even finished with their education yet. Why would they make a demand for teenagers to go to Germany?

It was suspicious.

The situation went even further out of control shortly after that first round of summonses.

The Nazis also began to send old people, young kids, and even orphans, off to "labor duty." That raised the hackles of everybody with a brain. Children? Orphans? Old ladies and old men? *Working?*

At *what?*

One of the Germans' claims to justify what they were doing with adding children to the transports was that they were endeavoring to "keep Jewish families together" in the "work camps." That didn't add up, not when it was revealed that orphans were being sent away, too.

Wherever they were all being sent, it was becoming harder and harder to believe the deportees would be put to industrious good use once they got there. Those summonses seemed to be some kind of a ruse.

A lie.

Lots of folks thought so, Charlotta reported to her hidden charge.

But finding proof of it was a whole other matter. And who in Holland could prove what was going on at the work details when they were supposedly taking place in Germany?

As a result of realizing there was something suspect about labor duty, many of the individuals who received summonses didn't bother

to show up on the designated days when they were supposed to be
shipped off, as a result.

This was smart on behalf of the Jews, but disastrous for the enraged
Nazis, who weren't one bit happy about it. They wanted the Jews out
of Holland. *All* of them. One official even said the country would be
"judenrein" within a year!

Judenrein meant "free of Jews."

Rika turned fifteen at the end of July. She didn't feel like celebrating
her birthday, but her brothers had other ideas. When they went up
to her room that night they had a small cake with them, courtesy of
Charlotta, who had managed to make it for her with sugar and butter
she'd purchased on the black market.

Outside, it was getting more unsatisfactory by the day. The Nazis'
legion of investigators had begun scurrying around, like rats, in an
attempt to hunt down all of the no-shows who did not show up for
deportation. They had their names on lists and wanted to ship to them
away, too.

To the Reich?

Really?

Or were they actually going someplace else?

Charlotta told Rika that rumors abounded about Poland.

All anyone knew for sure was that the Jewish people who left the
Netherlands were not heard from again. Even their closest non-Jewish
friends didn't hear a single peep out of them.

No letters, no postcards.

No word.

That included Julius Spranger. Bram Van Der Graaf had heard
from one of his contacts that Julius had, first, been in police custody,
until he got shipped away, too, at the beginning of July.

By the end of September, his children were still there, hidden in the
theater, and Bram hadn't heard anything from Julius yet. Not a single
word.

This struck him as beyond bizarre.

It was not like Julius.

The two of them had vowed to go through this mess of a war together, with Bram determined to assist Julius and his children in weathering the Nazi storm in any way he could. It was the whole reason why Bram had bought Julius' apartment from him, and the bookstore as well, so that at least on paper, they were no longer owned by a Jewish man, and were safe from Nazi confiscation.

Nikolaas had been strategically placed to run the bookstore, and Julius had promised Bram, back when he thought he was about to move to Naaldwijk, that once he got settled, he would find some way to keep in touch. "Maybe I'll sign my notes to you as being from 'Uncle Dolphi,'" he had even joked. "Dolphi," like a nickname for Adolph, as in Hitler, that was the punch line.

Yet there had been no communications from Julius at all.

Not a thing came in the mail from him to Bram, and nothing arrived signed "Uncle Dolphi," either. Bram wished something would.

No words or letters were passed along through intermediaries.

This was something Bram didn't tell the Spranger kids for fear of upsetting their limited world even further, but he was inwardly quite sick about it himself.

It did not bode well.

———◆———

BETJE VAN BEEK, THE ticket seller, couldn't figure out what had suddenly gone sour in her long friendship with Charlotta.

They had known each other for over a decade. Charlotta was her closest friend and had been ever since they had met as neighbors at their apartment building. They even both had a daughter about the same age. Betje's Lisette had been born almost a year earlier than Charlotta's Emmi. Lisette was also bigger and taller than Emmi, so whenever she outgrew a dress with a lot of wear left in it, Betje would give it to Charlotta so she could hand it down to her daughter.

When Betje's husband had suddenly died of a heart attack seven years earlier, Charlotta had immediately offered Betje the job of working the box office at the theater. It had solved Betje's financial problems of how in the world she was going to support her daughter and herself without a husband. She had believed that absolutely nothing in the world would ever have the force to come between herself and Charlotta.

Yet something had, apparently, gone very wrong.

Charlotta had always been so warm and friendly, but now she was different, somehow.

Furtive, like.

Betje thought, at first, it had something or other to do with the occupation, but then she thought maybe not.

She noticed Charlotta had taken to carrying a large cloth bag filled with something or other in and out of the theater, in addition to her small pocketbook.

Matters changed between the two friends on the day when Betje and Charlotta were leaving the theater at the same time. The bag, at the end of the day, looked almost empty, with only a rolled-up newspaper sticking out from the top of it. That wasn't how Charlotta had brought the thing into the theater that morning. Betje had seen Charlotta with it that day, and on other days. She always arrived with it full and bulging, so she couldn't resist making a comment.

She asked Charlotta just what she was toting around every day in such a large bag.

Charlotta got flustered. "What, this? The bag?" She stalled.

"Ja," replied Betje in a teasing way, yet puzzled at the evasive answer. "That. The *bag.*" She grinned at Charlotta but the pointed look on her face that she gave her had very little warmth in it.

She was challenging her, and Charlotta knew it.

Charlotta tried to shrug it off. "Oh, just some lunch for Bram and me. That's all."

It wasn't all, though she could not say so to Betje. It was the provisions for the three kids in hiding. The ones she managed to get for them with a little help from several forged ration cards.

"If you say so," Betje replied huffily.

She did not believe it.

She also didn't realize that her observance of the bag was the reason why Charlotta started to pull back from their friendship.

Betje was left puzzled about it. She decided to keep an eye on Charlotta in order to figure out what was going on with her. Maybe she was dealing on the black market.

Or...*something.*

———⊛———

ONE LATE OCTOBER NIGHT, Henk, Kees, and Rika were sitting in a row of seats in one of the balcony boxes, sharing slices of an apple that Charlotta had brought them earlier that day, and having a chat.

"What I'd like to know," Kees said, "is who exactly is this Joep Alderink? The one who pretended to be an identity card forger and set up Papa."

"I'm not sure," Henk replied. "Though I can't help but think that I've heard his name before. Somewhere." He shook his head, hoping to clear it and come up with the answer of where.

It didn't work.

"Think," urged Rika. The same question had been plaguing her since the day they found out their father was arrested.

"I'm trying that, and it isn't working," Henk answered her.

"Where could you have ever been that you might have heard the name of some Nazi?" Rika persisted. "And such a name as his, too. Joep Alderink. I would say it's rather unforgettable."

"My brother is already going senile in his old age," Kees joked.

"I'm not old," Henk grumbled. "I'm just stumped on where I heard it."

"I don't recall any Alderinks at our old school," Kees said thoughtfully.

"Neither do I," admitted Henk. "But there's still something about it. *Familiar.*"

It was Rika who finally came up with the answer, and she was simply guessing it. "You were friends with that Dutch Nazi's son. Petrus Prins," she reminded him. "Maybe did you hear any mention of this Alderink fink when you were anywhere near him?"

"Yes," Henk replied excitedly, realizing it, "actually, yes! I think so! Now that you mention it."

Henk thought of one of the last times he had seen Petrus. He was no longer welcome in the Prins house, of course, not with that Nazi father Petrus was stuck with issuing loud decrees against Henk's presence. He had once heard the father bellowing, "You keep that Jew to hell out of here!"

Yet Petrus' dad hadn't been able to get rid of Henk when he was talking to Petrus on the square of their street. Papa Prins may have wanted to own the whole street in its entirety, the green and all, and decree who could and couldn't be there, but he didn't, so he couldn't.

His son had been conversing with Henk one day a few months before the Sprangers had gone into hiding, discussing nothing major, just asking about Henk's new Jewish school. Petrus' father came out of the house along with his wife and had said, "Come on, Petrus. We're going to visit Joep Alderink and his wife."

Henk relayed this to his brother and sister now.

"If only," said Kees, "we could get in touch with Petrus now. He might be able to tell us something about Joep Alderink."

"Yes," agreed Henk, "but at the moment, that's impossible, isn't it?"

"For us," said Rika. "But maybe it wouldn't be out of the question for Nikolaas Van Der Graaf to ask Petrus?"

"Now there," nodded Henk, "is a fine idea."

"Of course it is," Kees agreed. "You know our sister is brilliant."

At that, Rika beamed.

―――――◉―――――

AS IT TURNED OUT, NIKOLAAS Van Der Graaf already knew Petrus Prins. They were not the same age, but still, they had grown up around the corner from one another. They had even attended the same school, though they'd been in different grades.

But before Nikolaas had a chance to try and pump Petrus for information about Joep Alderink there was another problem.

A bigger one than any of them had ever had since the whole hiding-in-the-theater situation began.

Chapter Eight

November 1942
Amsterdam, The Netherlands

OUTSIDE THE WIND WAS howling. Rika could hear it. The weather out there must be atrocious today, she thought.

Inside of the room that had been stiflingly hot in the summer, she was becoming increasingly chilled during the cold days of this late wartime autumn. Her room didn't come with a wood-burning stove or heater.

She would have to ask Bram and Charlotta to see if they could bring her an extra blanket, or better yet, two. She also was still wearing her summer dresses. Those would no longer do. Were some of her other outfits still in the apartment that Nikolaas now occupied, and could he possibly bring her a few winter items, like her favorite thick pink woolen sweater and maybe some mittens, too?

Any additional layer, she believed, would be a big help.

She wondered where her bright orange scarf was at the moment. Was that in the apartment? She would have loved to have it. On the other hand, if Nikolaas brought it over to the theater and happened to be stopped and searched by the Nazis, that could end badly. She wouldn't ask Charlotta to request that Nikolaas get it to her no matter how much she wished she could.

Charlotta told Rika the latest.

The Nazis had expanded on another one of their tactics, and it was being levied against the Dutch population as well as the Jews. They were rounding up more and more Dutch men to send to work as slave laborers in Germany. After all, they currently had a shortage of *German* men they could put to work in their own country. Their own able-bodied guys had almost all been conscripted into the Nazi armed forces.

This was odd. Hadn't thousands of Jews already been shipped off to work in Germany? Weren't they enough? Why did the Nazis need to add a bunch of Dutch men into the mix?

Whatever was going on, that's what they were doing. They'd first sent men off to work camps back during the riot in February, where the Dutch Nazi had been killed and a cop got injured, but more and more, Charlotta told her, were being sent away from Holland.

Rika hated to so much as hear that Nikolaas was out on the streets for any reason. It was increasingly dangerous for a young man to simply walk around.

I'm not the only one who isn't free around here, Rika thought. It's reaching the point where *nobody* is.

If only the Dutch Resistance people would step up and find a way to overthrow the Nazis! Or if the Allies, the Americans, French, British and Canadians, and the rest of the countries opposing Hitler, Mussolini and Hirohito, could do something to drive the accursed Nazis out of her, back over the border to where they came from! Or *something*.

If anything happened to Nikolaas because Rika needed warmer clothes she thought she would never be able to forgive herself.

Charlotta was fine with the request when Rika made it, and said she'd be happy to relay it to her son. A day later she knocked on Rika's door with the exact sweater the girl had wanted, a light blue scarf, and two heavier, woolen dresses. Rika had never been so happy so see anything in her life as she was to receive those warm items. A few days later Charlotta also managed to bring her some additional blankets, these coming from the De Graaf's apartment.

The theater itself was warmer than Rika's little room. There was always some heat in the auditorium. There had to be, or the audience would have stayed home in the colder weather.

Rika was cozier in her hiding place during the day with the addition of her good old winter clothing, but she was more than delighted to emerge every night, after the theater closed and emptied out. Usually one or both of her brothers came looking for her and brought her downstairs with them. They would sit in the empty auditorium, where there was still a trace of heat, and talk for hours.

Sometimes they even ran around, with a few overhead lights on, up one aisle of the theater and down the other, in order to get some exercise. They did jumping jacks. Rika remembered how much she'd loved playing hopscotch as a child, and sometimes leapt around the main center aisles, just as if she was following a hopscotch grid.

What fun, she was thinking on the night in November when the situation began to go wrong, it would be to be young again, playing games on the street! This, even though at the moment she was still a grand total of only fourteen years old. She didn't feel fourteen. More like a hundred. But it was enjoyable, almost, to put herself in mind of being seven or eight again and going through the motions of playing a game like hopscotch.

As she was doing that, Henk and Kees were sitting on the edge of the stage, in front of the movie screen, and discussing the latest reports on the newest newsreel that they'd managed to overhear in their dressing room. They weren't being loud, and neither was Rika. The center aisle was carpeted, and Rika was in her stocking feet, so her jumping and hopping wasn't creating more than a muffled noise.

But she happened to jump in the wrong place.

Actually, under the unprecedented circumstances of that particular night, there wouldn't have been any *right* place for her to be playing, but the three Sprangers didn't realize that.

"What the hell is *that?*" A voice roared from within a nearby aisle of seats.

Rika stopped dead in her tracks.

The two boys sitting on the stage jumped out of their skins, bug-eyed at the sound.

A hefty man sat up in one of the seats.

Who was this?

He had been slumped down, fast yet silently asleep, and the others had not noticed him there, since he was where he wasn't supposed to be in the first place. Paolo, the usher from Spain, usually made sure that the theater was cleared of audience members every night before he went home.

How had this one given Paolo the slip?

The man stood up. He was portly, with a beer belly, and his eyes were bloodshot.

He's drunk, Rika thought. Maybe he was sleeping it off here.

"Who are all of you?" The man roared.

As if he had any right to, considering he wasn't supposed to be there in the first place.

Rika thought fast. "We work here. You should have left already."

"Don't tell me what I should do or shouldn't do," came the belligerent reply. "If I want to stay here tonight, I will."

"The theater is closed," Henk informed him sharply.

"And you work here, too, do you?" The man asked. "Not likely! You look like a Jew. You people are not employable anymore."

That shut Henk up fast. He was shocked. He and Kees both had the dark hair that often went along with Jewish origins, and he didn't like it that this stranger had figured out his background with a single bloodshot-eyed look.

At least Rika didn't have dark hair, so she spoke up. "Don't you say that to him! He's a member of the Dutch Reformed Church, just like me." She added wildly, "He had an Italian grandmother." Italians usually had dark hair, too.

"Oh yeah? If he's an Italian then I'm Queen Wilhelmina," the drunk scoffed. "Does the other Jew sitting up there have an Italian grandma too?"

This wasn't good.

"You have to leave, sir," Rika replied, giving the order as firmly as if she was a cop.

The man looked at his watch. "No I don't. It's past curfew. I'm not going anywhere until the morning, and that's all that there is to that." He plopped back down in his seat. "And I don't take orders from Jews."

"We're not Jews," Rika lied.

"You're Jews, and you're liars," the man said in disgust. He removed a flask from his pants pocket and took a sip. He'd be drunker in no time. "I'm staying."

Kees took charge of his brother and sister. For the moment he said, but did not really mean, "Let him stay. He's right. He can't go out when it's past the curfew or the Nazis might arrest him for violating it."

"That's right," said the man.

"We missed curfew, too," Rika claimed. "There was a problem with the equipment, and we were trying to fix it, and it took too much time."

"Oh really? What kind of equipment could a bunch of young ones like you work on around here?" Without waiting for an answer he added, "You're lying Jews."

Kees commanded, "You two, *Marit and Jopie*, come with me."

"Ha! Their names can't possibly be Marit and Jopie," the man laughed and took another swig from his booze flask. Those were Dutch nicknames. For "Mary," or rather, "Maria," and "Joseph."

Rika wanted to yell, "Prove it!" But she didn't dare. That would only make it worse.

Kees saw his sister was about ready to explode and grabbed Rika's hand, pulling her toward the front of the auditorium to the backstage area, with Henk following behind.

"What do we do?" Rika whispered, as soon as they got back there.

"What we're not supposed to do unless there's an emergency," Kees replied. "Remember? We have to call Bram, tell him to come here right away, and have him get rid of that monster. Usher his fat ass out."

"It's not a good idea," Henk told him. "No one is supposed to be here at this hour. So if there's a phone call from here, where no one should be, to Bram's apartment, and *they* get wind of it, there's trouble!"

He didn't have to explain to the other two who he meant when he said "they." The Nazis. It was said they monitored the mail, telegrams, phone calls, everything.

"Well, we can't just leave that drunk out there," Rika lamented. Whispering, she added, "He's onto us."

"No he's not, *Marit,*" grinned Kees.

That was Kees. Always joking, even now. Yet this was not funny.

"Let him prove your name isn't Marit," Kees added now. "He can't. Don't you see?"

"I see this is dangerous," Rika replied. "That's what I see."

"I'm going into Bram's office and calling him at home," Kees announced, barreling on. "We can always say that that drunk out there went into his office and made the call himself, if it comes down to it and there's a question of who was in here using the phone. We'll say he got locked in and called Bram because he wanted to be let out."

Rika nodded, but wasn't even sure what she was agreeing with. Her heart was pounding a mile a minute.

They entered Bram's office, and closed and locked the door behind them.

Kees picked up the telephone and, with hands that were now shaking, dialed.

Chapter Nine

November 1942
Amsterdam, The Netherlands

———◆———

BRAM, TIRED AFTER A long day, had just sat down to a late dinner with Charlotta and their daughter Emmi when the telephone rang.

He sighed, since he had yet to eat the first bite of the dumplings his wife had prepared, and got up to answer it.

"Hallo?"

"Bram, it's me, Kees." The voice on the other end was whispering.

"Kees!" Bram exclaimed, before he could stop himself. His daughter previously had known nothing whatsoever about the three hidden teens, and he didn't want her to find out now, but the phone was in the hallway right next to their dining room.

She had probably heard.

Not good.

He asked, "What's going on?"

"There's a drunk who was sleeping in the theater. He saw all three of us. He guessed."

"I'll be right there," Bram replied. "Lock yourselves in your room," he added, now speaking in a whisper, so that, hopefully, Emmi wouldn't hear it.

But she had heard something. "Who was that? Was it Kees Spranger?" She asked brightly as soon as Bram poked his head back into the dining room.

"What? No! No, it's a new neighbor who lives above one of the shops on the theater's street," Bram told her, lying on the spot. As tall tales went, that was actually a believable one. Several shops on the street, the ones owned by Jews, had been taken over by new people, ones the Nazis favored. "It's a different guy named Kees. Ladies, I have to go over there to check something out and I'll be back soon."

"It's past curfew," Emmi pointed out. "You can't go!"

"You certainly can't," added Charlotta, though she said it with dread in her heart. What could be happening at the theater for Kees Spranger to have called Bram at home? It must be, had to be, something bad. She adored the three children who were secreted in the theater, sure, but didn't want Bram's life, or her own, to be put in jeopardy for them any more than they were already. It was nerve-wracking.

And where would Emmi wind up if both of her parents were arrested for hiding those kids?

Emmi, age eleven, was watching her parents closely. Her pretty mother's pale complexion had gone white, and her father was jittery and agitated. She was an observant girl, and her parents had been acting sneakily for months now.

She rarely missed a trick, and her father was lying.

So something was up.

"It's probably nothing," he said now, despite the fact that his words sounded lame even to his own ears, let alone to Emmi's. What could he come up with to explain this? "It's a vandal. That's what. With some paint. Probably trying to write 'oranje boven' or 'God save the queen' on the front of the theater, or something else that will annoy the Nazis. I'm going to go there, see what's what." He went to the door, grabbed his coat and hat off the rack, and slammed out of the apartment before his wife and daughter could try and stop him. He heard Charlotta cry out the word "no" as he left.

A man stayed at the theater and saw the kids! It was a terrible, and terrifying, development.

"Whatever happened to Kees Spranger?" Emmi asked her mother, who was staring in the direction of the shut door in shock.

"Oh, Kees? I am not sure," Charlotta lied uneasily. "Nobody is. The Spranger children were here one day, gone the next, right after their father was arrested." She spoke too rapidly.

"Rounded up?" Emmi asked. She fixed her green eyes steadily on her mother's blue ones. *Don't lie to me*, her expression conveyed, though Charlotta ignored it. She had no choice but to lie to her.

Charlotta, for her part, felt a pang in her chest at the whole idea of her eleven-year-old using language about a round-up as if it were the most commonplace thing in the world in the first place. What an awful concept for her child to be subjected to, and have knowledge of, during this current vile environment, and all because of this hideous war and the German invasion! It was yet another grievance she planned to hold against those damn Nazis.

"Emmi, darling. We just *don't know." She said it rather harshly, even the "darling."* Then, suspecting her tone of voice had gone too far, she added warmly, "They're missing. We just have to hold out, see what happens, and hope the Sprangers will all be back home someday, and soon, dear."

Emmi didn't buy that line for a minute. It's what people said about her little friend Hanni, who used to go to her school before the Jewish children were tossed out, too. Hanni lived down the street. She, her parents, and her brother had been "missing," which seemed to mean "sent away," for over a month, and there had been no word of them at all.

It was bad enough that her absolute best friend of all time, Verena Spranger, had gone to America and never came back, but at least she had written once in a while, until America entered the war and the mail between their two countries was stopped. Verena's little brother, another pal of Emmi's, was in America, too, and so was their mother, the kind lady she used to call Aunt Florentine, even though she wasn't really her aunt.

The other three Spranger kids had remained here.

Until they didn't.

Still. Emmi had to wonder about this phone call her father had just received.

From somebody who just happened to be called "Kees," yet.

———◉———

BRAM VENTURED OUTSIDE and found himself in the middle of a freezing-cold drizzling rain, bordering on sleet. He pulled the brim of his hat down lower over his eyes and made haste to walk the four blocks to the theater, hoping he wouldn't be stopped by some overzealous Nazi on patrol.

A blackout had been put into effect in the Netherlands, starting right away in May 1940, as soon as the blasted Germans had first taken over the country. It was done so that Allied aerial bombers would have a hard time navigating. If no lights were visible over Amsterdam, they couldn't see they were flying above the city. As a result, regulation blackout curtains had covered every single window, and no lights were visible anywhere.

This made his short illegal walk feel even creepier, and would have even if there *wasn't* the threat of some Duitser arresting him for being out and on the move after curfew.

On the other hand, so much total darkness made it considerably easier for Bram to prowl along the deserted ebony black street and fade in with the shadows. Sometimes, like this time, there was a benefit to the blackout.

At least no Nazis are out tonight, he thought. Why would they be, if they could stay inside where it was warm, rather than come out in *this?* The rain was freezing, and it started solidifying, too, skipping over the stage of sleet and transforming straight into hail as the temperature dropped further.

Bram reached his theater's block, and was startled by what was happening further up the street. He could see some action, what looked like a man standing under an umbrella about two blocks away. Gestapo, maybe. There was a truck idling at the curb over there. People, maybe Jews, were probably going to be loaded into it.

He immediately slowed down, standing under an awning over the recessed doorway of a shoemaker's shop, and pressing himself against it.

Sure enough. It looked like more men had come out of a building up ahead and were forcing a few people into the truck, guns trained on them.

Bram waited.

The man with the umbrella lowered it and opened the door of the truck, the one next to the driver, and got in.

The truck sped away.

Bram hadn't realized that he was shaking until they were gone, and only then, his terror subsided.

Finally he proceeded to the alleyway that led to the courtyard behind the theater. There was no reason for him to go through the front door tonight. He'd go in the back.

"Hey there, Bram," a voice startled him from behind as he reached the movie theater's back doorway.

He jumped.

"Oh, Bram, relax. It's only me," came a woman's laugh out of the dark. "It's Corina."

Then he recognized her, and that was a relief. It was Corina Temmink, a woman who lived with her daughters in the next building. They had an apartment above her jewelry shop. She could be an annoying flirt, to both his and Charlotta's annoyance, and she wasn't a pleasant woman, but at least she wasn't another armed Nazi. Corina was standing in the dark, wearing a flimsy nightgown, in her open back doorway. It led to her apartment upstairs.

"I just wanted to see what Mother Nature was doing out here," she admitted. "All this hail. It's making a racket."

"Yes," Bram agreed congenially. "Yes, you're right, it is."

"Well, good night, Bram. Don't get caught," she added, then let out a cackle.

Bram didn't like the sound of it.

"I got a call there was a vandal lurking about," he replied defensively. "Thought I'd better not wait until morning to check on it and should get here right away."

"Oh, I wasn't asking," Corina replied, but in a lofty and knowing tone of voice, as if she had her suspicions about what he was doing and didn't buy his explanation for a minute. "Whatever you're here for, you're here for, and you're breaking the curfew. You know me. I'm not curious. Not these days. Good night, then, Bram."

"Good night, Corina." He kept his voice level, which took a bit of an effort, since he didn't like what she had just said, let alone the way she'd said it. He left her there, still silhouetted in her back doorway, looking out at the raucous hailstorm.

Bram finally was able to let himself into the theater. He went straight to the dressing room, knocking on the door two times. "It's me, Bram. Open up."

"Just a minute," he heard Kees say. From the other side of the door came a scraping sound. Once Kees opened it, Bram realized he had moved a table in front of the door in order to block it.

"We were afraid," Kees explained, "he'd try to come back here and break in."

Bram looked at the three of them. All of them looked terrified. Kees was clearly distressed, Henk looked anxious and was biting a nail, and Rika was sitting on the floor hugging her knees.

"Quickly! What did you tell him?" Bram asked them.

"That we work here, we missed curfew, and we're not Jews," said Henk. "The guy didn't believe it."

"Oh, this is not good," Bram breathed.

"I said their names were Marit and Jopie," Kees added.

"And I told him we're all members of the Dutch Reformed Church," Rika looked up and revealed.

"Okay. Let me handle the rest of this. You stay here, and for God's sake keep quiet until morning."

He closed the door and could heard Kees locking it behind him.

Who knew what he was going to find when he met the awful man in the auditorium?

Chapter Ten

November 1942
Amsterdam, The Netherlands

———◉———

CORINA TEMMINK HADN'T gone back inside her building.

She remained, instead, in the doorway.

It wasn't comfortable. Oh, she was wearing a long nightgown, but it was not the kind to provide the right amount of warmth or cover during a storm like this.

Even so.

She had known for quite some time that there was something going on in that theater of Bram's after hours. Nobody could tell her that there wasn't, although her latest boyfriend, the Lieutenant, accused her of "hearing things" whenever she tried to mention it.

That was nonsense. At least her boyfriend hadn't stayed over on this particular night. If he had, he would have stopped her from what she was about to do.

Too many people were not where they were supposed to be these days. Corina knew all about it. There were Jews who disappeared into hiding. There were men who did the same thing to avoid being sent to Germany on labor detail.

She wasn't sure who the people were that had taken up residence in the theater, whether they were Jewish and should have been deported, or Dutch and not inclined to go to work for the Germans, but *some people* were in there. She knew it. She'd known it since the October night when her little dog had gotten out, and curfew or no curfew, she had gone outside to chase him around the courtyard and tried to get him back into the house.

The dog had stopped in front of the dressing room window of the theater building.

Charlotta had told her once that that particular window was in an unused dressing room, left over from the days when the theater had featured live performances.

Corina no longer believed it. If that room wasn't used, why then would Charlotta have put up *blackout curtains* in there? Why bother? If no one really used it.

Then no one would have turned any lights on in there.

That meant someone probably did use it, though at first, Corina didn't suspect anything unusual was going on. For one thing, Charlotta had told her all that stuff about the room before the war started, prior to when so many people suddenly had reasons to try and make themselves invisible. It was only recently that she had to wonder about the installation of those blackout curtains.

Even at that, Corina didn't know realize anything was happening in there until that night back in October when the dog got loose.

It had been an evening similar to this one, only with pouring rain instead of this heavy hail. Her boyfriend hadn't spent that night with her, either. She had gone down the stairs to look out the back door just to see what the weather was doing and had not realized the dog, Grootje, was right behind her. They called him Grootje, "big one," as a gag, because he was a sweet-tempered, tiny poodle.

Grootje didn't like the curfew the Germans had imposed any more than any of the rest of the populace did. He missed the days when he could go outside at night and run around the courtyard, getting plenty of exercise. Corina was sure he was even rather proud of himself for sneaking out on her. Well, she couldn't blame him for that.

As far as she knew, there were no Nazis monitoring the courtyard, since it was behind the buildings on the street, but you never knew.

People were arrested all the time for violating the damned curfew. Yet what could she do except go out there and retrieve her dog? Surely not even the Nazis would have a problem with *that*? She knew enough not to announce it to anybody, but she actually happened to secretly admire most of the efforts of those Nazis. They were shipping the Jews away and good riddance, and they made good customers at her store, buying expensive presents to send to their sweethearts and wives back home. She was even friendly with the Lieutenant. Perhaps since she had no issue with them, they'd have none with her, just for going after Grootje, and that would only be *if* they saw her outside after hours on that October that night.

Grootje, after running around in the rain for a bit and remembering he didn't like it that much, looped around the courtyard, and came to a dead stop by the dressing room window. The dog stopped there, transfixed, but by what?

Corina went over to grab him and see what had caught the little dog's attention.

That's when she'd heard voices coming from inside of the room!

They weren't loud ones. It sounded like they belonged to some youngsters.

"Your turn to deal," one said. A boy.

"I'll beat you this time," came from another voice, along with a laugh. That sounded like it came from a girl.

"No you won't," said the first one. Or so she thought. It may have come from a second boy.

From that point on, Corina knew there were children hidden in that theater.

And, since they sounded young, it probably meant they were the children of her least favorite people.

Jews.

She had been paying attention to every single nuance going on at that movie theater ever since. She'd even gone to see films on a few

Sundays, when her shop was closed, just to take the place all in, and see whatever she might see. It hadn't led to any further information, but Corina was not going to stop looking.

Now this. That gorgeous Bram Van Der Graaf had shown up during a hailstorm, out of nowhere, after curfew, and she had caught him having to sneak into his own building. Scared him almost straight out of his shoes, too.

Oh, something was up!

So she left the door wide open, and, ignoring the cold and the storm, went over to that window. She put her ear to it.

Sure enough.

Bram was in there saying, "Quickly! What did you tell him?"

"That we work here, we missed curfew, and we're not Jews," said the voice of a boy. "The guy didn't believe it."

Aha!

She knew it!

Bram was hiding Jews!

———————⊙———————

BRAM HESITATED BEFORE going into the auditorium. What could he say to the dolt who was camping out in his theater?

I'll use the same excuse as the kids, he decided, and the one used by the twit who hadn't left the theater yet, too.

The curfew.

I can say I also stayed too late and had missed it, and will act like I've been here all along.

He took off his coat and hat and left them both, still soaking wet, on a chair backstage. It wouldn't do for him to claim he'd been inside all this time and go to see this stranger while looking drenched.

After that, he went in to find the guy, wondering just who he was. Kees had said he was a drunk, but what kind of drunk? Dutch? NSB? German? *Gestapo?*

It could be nothing, or might be dangerous. Like everything else these days.

It wasn't hard for Bram to find him. He was sitting in an upright position in one of the seats, with his arms folded, clearly visible under the overhead lights that the kids hadn't bothered to turn off after being in there, probably because they were too upset at finding this *idioot*.

"Hello there, sir," Bram called out to him, forcing himself to use a jovial tone. "Can I help you?"

"Yes, you can. You can pay me off," the large guy smiled. "You've got Jews hiding here." He was slurring his words. Either he was already drunk out of his mind or close to it.

"Like hell I do. I'm the owner. There are no Jews on the premises."

"You've got three of them, owner, and they pretend to work here when they don't," the man replied. "I've been here lots of times and never saw those three working here before."

"They're new hires," Bram ad-libbed. "They're not Jewish at all. They go to the same Dutch Reformed church as I do. It's getting cold in here, sir." That was because Bram didn't keep the heat on overnight. "I own this place, and it looks like all of us missed curfew tonight. Can I get you some schnapps? I could use some myself."

That changed his attitude. "Yes, now! Schnapps would be great!"

Bram knew he would say that. What drunk ever said no to another drink?

So far, so good.

"Just wait for a minute and I'll come back with two glasses and the bottle. We can talk."

"Negotiate, you mean," the large man cackled.

Bram stifled a sigh. It was going to be a long night.

———◉———

BRAM COULDN'T GET RID of the man until six o'clock in the morning. He was beyond exhausted by then, having been up all night, without having gotten any dinner, and only having put a little too much schnapps in his empty stomach while he kept the raising a glass with the *dronkaard.*

And *talking.*

He'd found out a lot about him, at least.

The man's name was Hannus Douw. He was a Dutchman, but a traitorous Nazi sympathizer, and he made no secret that he couldn't stand the Jews.

It took half the night for Bram to convince Douw that the three kids he had seen were not Jewish. This was the sort of man who would turn them in without a second thought, Bram knew, if he continued to believe they were of the Hebrew persuasion.

If he did that, the three Sprangers could end up shipped away, Bram and Charlotta would probably find themselves in a prison, and Emmi might be stuck living in an orphanage.

It had Bram scared half to death.

"I'm telling you, Hannus, those three young ones attend my church every week," he lied to Douw. "They recently lost both of their parents. The least I felt I could do was give them a little job here and try to help them out." He added, "It's the Christian thing to do," all the while wondering if such a line might just be overdoing it.

"What if it's all just a fake story?" Hannus asked. "That they're orphans. You could get in trouble just for hiring Jews, let alone allowing them to stay in your theater at night."

"It isn't a lie. Not according to the pastor," Bram told him. "They're the pastor's cousins. And believe me, I didn't let them stay here overnight, any more than I gave permission for you to do so," Bram said pleasantly, as if this was all some kind of a lark. "But here you are and here they are. And here I am, too. But I must say, I'm actually glad that none of you went out on the street too late. It would have been dangerous for you otherwise."

That was another grand fib. The lies were getting bigger and wider by the minute, but Hannus was becoming drunker, and he looked as if he was starting to take Bram's words in.

It was five o'clock in the morning before Hannus admitted, "I didn't believe them. When the one boy said the others were called Marit and Jopie, I couldn't believe it wasn't a ruse."

"It isn't," Bram said. "Sorry to disappoint you, pal, but they're not Jewish."

"These days," Hannus replied, "ha! Nobody says they are. Even the ones who are, aren't. You can never really know who's who anymore. Let alone what's what."

"There's not a thing I can do about that," Bram replied with a forced laugh. "But before you leave, can I give you some movie passes? I've enjoyed our talks tonight and would be happy to see you here again."

That was the biggest line of nonsense of them all. The only way Bram would ever want to see this clown again would be if he was holding a club and could hit him over the head with it.

Chapter Eleven

November 1942
Amsterdam, Netherlands

———————◆———————

HANNUS DOUW FINALLY left the theater a little after six o'clock the next morning. Bram had never been happier to see anybody go out of a door in his life. He made sure he locked the door behind him.

Tired as he was, and concerned as he was about Charlotta and Emmi, since he hadn't made it home the evening before, he knew he had to get moving and find another option for the three teenagers who were hiding at his theater, and fast. The Sprangers were no longer safe there and that was all there was to it.

They would have to be moved.

Immediately, if not sooner!

Bram went to the dressing room, where all three of the kids, even Rika, had spent the whole night. "Rika," he told her, "I think you should go upstairs to your usual spot."

"I will," she said agreeably, "but how did it go?"

"Oh." Bram seemed to deflate in front of their eyes. "I think I convinced that horrible man, who by the way loves the Nazis, God help us, that you're my pastor's cousins and Protestants, but I don't like it. He's quite a drunk, and you know how unreliable they can be. He could have said he believed me while he was here, then go out to a bar, get soused, and announce he thinks I'm hiding Jews, after he has a few. It's time to move you along. I hate to have to do that, but at this point it's our only option. Don't be surprised if I have to split you up."

"We'll do what we have to do," Rika assured him. She was a great kid, always so positive about all of this insanity. If she didn't like the idea of being separated from her brothers, she never would have said it out loud.

How, Bram wondered, was he going to find three hiding places, one for each of them? The idea of looking for one seemed impossible enough. Three was going to be an uphill battle. Nobody ever advertised where those willing to hide Jews could be found. How could they? It wasn't legal to shelter them!

"Get your stuff together," he said now. "I'm going to get other places for you as soon as I can. You might have to leave without much warning."

With that, Rika went through the empty auditorium to the lobby, up to the balcony, and further, to her room across from the projectionist booth. The theater suddenly struck her as bleak.

Bram also left as Rika did. The boys locked the doors behind them.

Exhausted Bram dragged himself the four blocks home. He passed a Nazi soldier and gave him a nod hello, not that he wanted to greet him, just to try *not* to stand out by acting unfriendly.

It worked.

For the moment.

———◉———

CORINA TEMMINK HAD gotten herself drenched, all the way through her nightgown, the evening before, when she'd positioned herself by the old dressing room window and heard all the goings-on in that movie theater. It had been well worth it!

Bram Van Der Graaf, hiding Jews! It was wonderful! It might even finally give her a chance to get some revenge on Bram for always acting as if he was so far above her when he should have realized that he wasn't.

Bram was one of the few men who couldn't be moved by her wiles.

Charlotta was just as bad. She was so smug in her relationship with her husband.

Or at least, that's how it seemed to be in the twisted mind of Corina, who couldn't seem to understand that the Van Der Graafs had no interest in her.

Bram, in particular, didn't want to get involved with Corina, no matter how much she had flirted with him over the years, making it obvious what she would have been available to do, if only he wanted to comply. Bram secretly thought she had the kind of morals that could have led her straight to the Amsterdam red light district, had she been so inclined, and if she hadn't inherited her late husband's jewelry shop. There was always a boyfriend going in and out of Corina's building. It had happened at all hours of the day and night before the war, and still went on now, although these days it conformed to the timing of the damned curfew.

Bram was not thinking of Corina as he made his way home to Charlotta and Emmi. He had not realized she'd had her ear to the window the night before, or that she'd been suspicious of what was going on in the theater for a month already, thanks to her infernal dog, Grootje.

But Bram was on Corina's mind. She had two daughters who had two different fathers, neither one of which had been Corina's husband, though he hadn't known it when he was alive and had been supporting them. One of them was in the same class as Emmi Van Der Graaf. Corina zeroed in on that one, Kornelia, that morning.

"Neeltje," she said to her, using Kornelia's nickname, with a wolflike smile as she made the girls their porridge. "You haven't brought Emmi Van Der Graaf over to play in a long time. Why don't you ask her to come by this afternoon?"

Neeltje glanced at her mother. She was no fan of Corina. There was an edge to her mother that she did not like. The girl missed her father, who had been in the Dutch Army, and had died in battle when the Germans invaded.

Or, at least, she missed the man she *thought* was her father, not knowing that he wasn't. He had been normal and steady and responsible.

Corina was anything but.

"Why?" She asked her mother skeptically.

"Oh, you know, Neeltje. It's good to have friends. We haven't seen Emmi around here in ages."

"Emmi got to be good friends with Hanni the Jew, until she got kicked out of school. They were always together, and now Hanni's gone. Rumor has it she got taken away." Neeltje took a spoonful of her porridge. If her mother wanted her to bring Emmi home, she vowed, she would *not* invite the girl over. She knew from the glint in Corina's eyes that her mother was up to something.

Corina's other daughter, Lena, emerged from her room at that point, and also sat down to breakfast. She was older than her sister, and liked her mother a lot more than Neeltje did, but she wasn't blind to Corina's manipulations, either. "What are you talking about?" She asked.

"Simply that your sister hasn't had Emmi Van Der Graaf come over to play in a long, long while," Corina answered, trying to put a look of innocence into her eyes.

Neeltje shot Lena a look and rolled her eyes.

"Oh *Moeder*, can't you let Neeltje decide for herself who she wants to pal around with?" Lena suggested.

"Yes, can't you?" Neeltje added with a grin. She loved the way Lena always backed her up.

"I wasn't trying to interfere," Corina protested.

"Much," said Neeltje, and tried to go back to eating her breakfast.

"Perhaps you would be interested to know this, though," Corina went on sweetly. "They're hiding Jews over there in the movie theater next door, those Van Der Graafs are."

"So that's why you want Emmi to come over here," Lena laughed. "You want *informatie.*" Information.

"Well, yes. Of course! Don't you want to find out more?" Corina asked.

Her two daughters looked at one another again. Hiding Jews. It was a rather daring and exotic thing to do.

So the answer to that was yes.

They did want to learn more about it.

Even so, Neeltje still didn't want to invite Emmi over. And she wouldn't.

<hr />

BRAM ARRIVED HOME, and wanted nothing more than to get some much-needed sleep. He'd never had such a nerve-wracking night.

He couldn't just go straight to bed, however. Not with the threat of Hannus Douw's knowledge of Rika, Henk and Kees hanging over his head.

Charlotta and Emmi were thrilled and relieved to see him come in through the door.

"Bram! I've been up all night and worried sick! What happened?" Charlotta rushed to him, threw her arms around him and asked.

"Papa, I was so afraid! When you didn't come home I thought they'd taken you," Emmi added, also giving her father a great big hug.

"You two," he smiled. "You should have realized I wasn't going to come home until the end of the curfew."

"We didn't know what you were planning to do, to be honest," Charlotta told him. *"What happened?"*

Bram just gave her a look. It wouldn't do to discuss the latest developments in front of Emmi. The less she knew, the better.

"It was a long night," was all he said. "I want to have some breakfast, and then I have to get some rest. All's well," he added, telling a lie yet again, this time for his daughter's benefit.

"But what went on?" Emmi wanted to know. "Did you catch the vandals?"

Bram almost asked her *what vandals* until he remembered that that was the story he'd given to the child the night before to cover the fact that the Sprangers were discovered. "False alarm on that, but then I got stuck there," he replied. "You're not to worry about it."

Emmi wasn't satisfied with his answer. Why were her parents constantly acting so suspiciously these days? Was it possible they were in the Dutch Resistance? Or just what exactly did they have going on?

As for Bram, he could not wait until his daughter went off to her school. He had some tea and toast, and when Emmi went into the bathroom, whispered to Charlotta, "I'm going to lie down as soon as I finish this, but if I fall asleep, wake me up the second Emmi goes out the door. We have to talk."

<hr />

RIKA WASN'T SURE WHAT to feel when she got back to her hideaway.

On the one hand, it would be fantastic to get out of here. To not have to live in the dark all day and only emerge at night to roam the inside of the theater. To live somewhere else, in the light.

On the other hand, at least in the dark she could listen to movies, which was almost fun. She was in good hands with Bram and Charlotta. She could be with her brothers every night when the patrons went home.

It was all out of her hands now, though. Where would she go? Would she be safer there, wherever it was? The thoughts made her anxious.

She had dutifully kept all of her possessions, as few as they were, in the duffel bag, all in one place, ready to go, the way she'd been instructed to do. She had spent the whole night in one of her dresses without changing into a nightgown, so now she changed out of that one and put her other dress on.

Would she be leaving today? She dreaded it, yet hoped so, both at the same time.

———— ◉ ————

"HI, JEW LOVER!"

That was how Neeltje Teemink greeted the unsuspecting Emmi when she arrived that morning at the schoolyard.

"How's tricks, Jew lover?" Lena added, standing over Emmi and laughing in her face.

"Why are you calling me a Jew lover?" Emmi shot right back. She had nothing against Jews. Verena was Jewish, Aunt Florentine and Uncle Julius, Kees, Henk, Rika, Hanni – so many of her favorite people. All of them were gone now, one way or the other.

But as young as she was, she realized it wasn't a good idea, these days, to say too much in favor of the members of that particular religion, since the Nazis had so many regulations against them. And Nazis couldn't be counted on to act decently around anyone who disagreed with their nonsense.

"You know why," Neeltje taunted her.

"Yes, you know exactly," Lena nodded with a smug look on her face.

"You should tell us all the details," Neeltje added. "Why play dumb? We know what your parents are hiding. And we know where, too."

"Right. Next. Door," Lena taunted her.

Emmi looked from one of the sisters to the other. What did they mean? What they were saying didn't make any sense.

Not yet, at least.

The bell rang at that point, stopping the strange discussion in its tracks.

That was when she remembered the phone call of the night before. The one from "Kees."

How her father had said it wasn't from Kees Spranger, but how she'd wondered if that was for real or not.

The way he had run out in the storm to go to the theater.

And how he had not come back until this morning.

Could this have something to do with that?

It could.

Yes, she thought as she ran down the hallway of the school to get to class, it definitely could, especially when you considered these two horrible Teemink girls lived in the building right next door.

If her parents were hiding Jews, that's probably where they were stashing them. There was plenty of room where people could be hidden in that big theater.

She had to wonder, as she sat down at her desk in her classroom, how she could find out more about whatever was going on. Her mother and father, she already knew, would never, ever tell her. It also wouldn't be a good idea to ask that awful Neeltje. If what Emmi suspected was true, her parents could end up in major trouble if anyone found out what they were doing.

That's if they were actually hiding people. Which was a big "if" to Emmi at the moment, even as it did seem likely.

She thought of Paolo, the young guy from Spain who worked at the theater as an usher, who also cleaned the aisles between shows, and did all of the handyman stuff that was sometimes required around the place. Emmi got along well with Paolo.

After school she'd go to the theater as usual and see if she could get Paolo to tell her what he knew.

She had no way of knowing that, so far, Paolo hadn't known anything about it, and wouldn't.

Until she told him.

Chapter Twelve

November 1942
Amsterdam, Netherlands

———◦———

BRAM HAD FALLEN ASLEEP the moment his head hit the pillow in the bedroom he shared with Charlotta.

She remained in the dining room with her daughter, and waited until half an hour later, when Emmi had all but skipped out the door to school. Charlotta wished she didn't have to wake her poor husband up. He was clearly fatigued, and that was never good.

But there was a problem. She could tell.

And it was huge.

She went into the bedroom and woke him with the optimistic saying, *"Opstaan en stralen, Bram!"* It meant get up and shine.

She had to repeat it twice until he was roused from sleep. "Ah. Shine. Yes, wouldn't that be a fine idea?" Bram mumbled.

At that point, he remembered the events of the previous day, and sat right up in the bed.

"Emmi's off to school. So what happened?" Charlotta asked desperately.

"The worst thing possible, that's what. A drunk by the name of Hannus Douw didn't leave the theater at closing time last night. I wouldn't be surprised if he'd had too much to drink before he got there and was sleeping it off in one of the seats. Whatever happened, he missed curfew, and he stayed, sleeping. The kids thought the place was vacant, came down into the theater, and accidentally woke him up. Right away he pegged the boys as Jewish."

"Oh my God," breathed Charlotta.

"Your God can't help you here, and neither can theirs. I had a terrible time trying to convince him that they weren't, but can't be certain if he believed me or not. Charlotta, he's a reprobate. He's pro-Nazi. I'm terrified he'll get drunk somewhere and start blurting out his suspicions of what we've got going on in the theater, and I don't mean on the screen. We have to move those kids out of there at once."

"But where can they go?" Charlotta asked.

"I don't know! I'm not even sure who we should ask for a referral, as it were, for a new hiding place. We just have to get them out of there right away. Now."

"We can't have them stay here," Charlotta said.

"Of course not! With Emmi around? And compromise her? Never."

"Maybe it would be possible for Nikolaas to keep them for a few days," Charlotta mused. "What do you think? The Nazis were not happy when they went over to the Spranger's apartment and found out it had already been sold to you, and we've put Nikolaas in there. But they wouldn't think to go back there to look for those three, knowing their father had sold the place to someone else."

"Short term, that might just work," Bram agreed. "You're a genius! But long term, we still have to find a different accommodation for them. I don't want Nikolaas compromised."

"I don't either. It's bad enough we got ourselves into this dilemma," Charlotta told him.

"It will be worth it in the end," Bram assured her, "when the war is over and Kees, Henk and Rika are alive and well and able to live freely again. We can send them to America, to their mother. Maybe Julius will even return from wherever it is he's been sent and can go there with them."

Charlotta just shook her head sadly at that. She hoped it would happen, but what were the odds?

———●———

EMMI HAD NEVER HAD a worse day at school.

Neeltje went after her at recess, and also managed to get two more children, bratty friends of hers, to chase after her. All of them were yelling a whole lot of garbage and insults, saying Emmi and her parents were committing a crime by hiding Jews and that all three of them ought to be arrested. And more.

Finally Emmi turned around and screamed, "You're all just a bunch of Nazis, that's what you are! Nazis! Dutch Nazis! That makes you nothing but traitors! You wouldn't be saying these things otherwise!"

She was surprised to see that was enough to shut them up.

After that, a teacher intervened, leading Emmi to a corner of the playground, away from Neeltje and her ilk.

Strangely, no teacher arrived to take on Neeltje. The worst of the students, the bullies, always seemed to *"Ergens mee wegkommen."* Get away with something. There wasn't even any point complaining that it wasn't fair. It just wasn't and that was it.

The day seemed like it would never be over, but once it was, the girl headed for the theater.

Charlotta and Bram always asked Emmi to come to the theater right after school let out, since both of them were always busy working there every day. So that's where she was headed once the dismissal bell rang.

Vicious Neeltje and her older sister, equally evil Lena, walked in the same direction, of course, since their place was next door to the theater. Emmi hung back for some time, wandered into a small park with the usual "no Jews allowed" sign, VOOR JODEN VERBODEN, and sat down on a bench that would have been banned to children like her missing friend Hanni. She wanted to give Neeltje a head start and not have to encounter her on the street.

Not for a moment did Emmi consider the fact that it might be a rather bad idea to find out if Paolo knew what was going on.

Her parents trusted him completely, didn't they? He *had to* know, and he would tell her.

Wouldn't he?

She was sure of it.

———————◦———————

CHARLOTTA WAS NOWHERE to be found that afternoon, once Emmi arrived at the theater.

The child didn't know that her mother had taken Rika out of there an hour before school let out. That way she wouldn't have to chance running into her daughter, who would have had a million questions, on the street, had she seen her with Rika.

It was not as miserable a day as the previous one had been. There wasn't any hail, or even rain, but still, it was cold and damp.

That was all to the good. Charlotta used the weather as an excuse to put the blue scarf that Nikolaas had found for Rika, when she'd asked for warmer clothes, around Rika's head, in order to make her harder to recognize by anyone on the street who might have known her before. She wore her summer coat, since she didn't have the winter one with her when she went into hiding, and her pink sweater underneath it, over a dress. The hat from her mother was on her head, coming with her. She would not leave that behind.

"Try to walk as if you've been out here every day," Charlotta said cheerfully to her charge as the girl was able to emerge from the theater as casually as if she'd never been imprisoned, so to speak, inside of it for so many months. They left amongst the crowd that was leaving an afternoon movie as if it was the most natural thing in the world.

Rika wished she could give a wave to Betje, who was in the box office, as she went past her, but did not dare. With the blue scarf around her head, topped by the hat from her mother, it was doubtful Betje would have recognized her anyway.

Rika knew better than to stare at the wonders of the street, but oh how she wished she could have! She longed to look in the window of Corina Temmink's jewelry shop, or the one at the notions store. She wanted very much to see what records were currently available at the music shop, which had once been one of her favorite stores. Actually, she wanted to take in absolutely everything, but just kept her eyes averted and walked with Charlotta, keeping a nice brisk pace.

She was surprised to find out that their destination was her old apartment.

The duo waited across the street while one of the other tenants of the building was emerging. He was an old man who would have recognized Rika. They didn't go inside with the key Nikolaas had earlier given to his mother until the man went on his way. That took longer than it should have because he walked with a cane.

Once safely inside the apartment, Charlotta explained what was going on. "We've got it all planned. Nikolaas will go to the theater and bring Emmi home to our apartment, after he closes up the book shop. Bram will come by here after that, with your brothers. We're trying to place you elsewhere, but it may take a little time, so for now, we doubt the Nazis would ever look for you here. They already came and went once they found out your father sold this place to us."

Rika looked around happily. It was so nice to be home! There was the sofa and her mother's favorite chair. The yellow kitchen with the white tile. Her pink bedroom that she had once shared with her little sister Verena. All her clothes were still in the closet! The idea of wearing a different outfit every day of the week appealed to her like it never had before. She had gotten used to switching off between two dresses only.

Charlotta reminded her to stay away from the windows, which were blocked by the blackout curtains anyway, while Rika decided to draw a bath. There were even some fragrant soap crystals, lilac, that were still on the bathroom shelf! She put them into the water and let the scent fill up the room.

The water was lukewarm, not as hot as it used to be, but after so many months of having to take what she thought of as a "half a bath," with a washcloth in the theater's rest room after the place closed for the night, she would take a bath any way she could get it. It was an amazing feeling to settle into the tub!

There was a bar of soap that she enormous took pleasure in using and even some old shampoo. All those months she had spent hiding in the theater, she had lathered her hair, rather unsuccessfully, with a regular bar of soap. The shampoo that she found in her old bathroom was a glorious sight to behold.

She didn't emerge for an entire fabulous hour.

———⊛———

"PAOLO," EMMI SAID, when she found the young man in the lobby of the theater, "would you know where my mother is?"

Paolo said he didn't. "I heard the boss, your father, say she was going home early. He said if I saw you that Nikolaas was going to be picking you up here tonight."

"Nikolaas?" The girl repeated. "Why would my brother have to come here and get me when my parents are here all the time?"

Paolo shrugged. "Maybe they have an engagement. Who knows? Your father is back in his office. You might want to ask him."

Emmi looked at this guy that she considered her friend. "Paolo. Can I ask you something?"

"*Naturlich,*" he replied. Naturally.

"Do you know," she asked, lowering her voice, "anything about my parents hiding some Jews?"

Paolo was startled at the question. "What?" He repeated. "No, Emmi. Of course not!"

It wasn't the reaction she expected.

"At school," she told him, "there's two girls who were saying things like that about my mother and father. They're the girls who live next door over the jewelry shop."

"People saying things doesn't make them true," Paolo reminded her, but what she said was upsetting to him. Jews, hiding here?

"The girls seemed pretty sure they knew what they were talking about," Emmi insisted.

"Two girls? They're probably making it up," Paolo replied, a little too loudly. "Your parents aren't hiding any Jews. They wouldn't do that here."

Paolo and Emmi didn't see who was also in the lobby at that particular moment.

It was Marijke, the girlfriend of the projectionist, Gustav De Boon. She overheard Paolo's statement about the owners of the theater hiding Jews. It almost stopped her dead in her tracks.

Gustav himself wasn't there with her, since he only worked on the weekends. The poor guy didn't know it, but he was only one of a whole endless string of boyfriends that Marijke had. She was about as picky where men were concerned as Corina Temmink.

Marijke had been crossing the lobby to get to the rest room because the current movie, and her latest guy, were both boring her to tears. He didn't even bother to hold her hand as they sat there in the dark!

Now she decided to go back to her seat, feign sick, grab her coat, and leave the theater.

If Gustav was working in a place where Jews might be hiding, she needed to warn him.

At once.

Chapter Thirteen

November 1942
Amsterdam, Netherlands

———◆———

EMMI DECIDED NOT TO mention her conversation with Paolo to her father when she went and found him in his office backstage.

All she asked him was, "Where's Mama?"

"Your mother went on an errand," Papa said, looking down at a document on his desk, and not up at her.

Lying to me again, she thought. Just because Paolo didn't think her parents were hiding Jews didn't mean that they really weren't. Maybe Paolo really didn't know about it, though that seemed impossible to Emmi. She always figured Paolo knew absolutely everything about the theater.

That's if Neeltje and Lena had given her accurate information in the first place.

"Oh, Nikolaas is coming by tonight to take you home," Bram told her now, finally meeting her eyes.

"Why can't you?" Emmi wanted to know.

Bram tried not to get exasperated with her. What the child didn't know wasn't her fault.

Even so, she could be trying at times. Like now.

All he cared about at the moment was getting the two boys out of this place and over to his son's apartment. It was vitally important, and more so than Emmi's questions. If he timed it right he could walk out with them, the same way Charlotta had left with Rika, along with the rest of the crowd at the end of the last movie. The newsreel was on at the moment. He could hear it. The movie still had yet to begin.

Waiting for it to end, when it had yet to begin, was enough to make Bram tense.

Now, to answer his daughter, he came up with, "I have to go to the bank for a few minutes before going home. Don't worry, Emmi. Just go with Nik when he comes. Get yourself something from the refreshment stand, too. You must be hungry after a long day at school."

"The longest one ever," Emmi said under her breath.

The little girl walked away from the office at that point, and at a fast clip.

She didn't realize how long it would be until she saw her father again. It was going to haunt her later, the memory of how she'd turned her back on Papa and had all but run out of there.

———◉———

MARIJKE HAD A HARD time getting away from that day's date, Eduard.

"Let me come with you," he all but begged, "let me see you home, at least, if you're sick!"

"No, I've, I'm, I need to get going, right now," Marijke had replied. "You stay here and watch the movie. You wanted to see it."

"Sssshh!" Some of the audience members sitting near them hissed.

Marijke finally made her escape.

Gustav had a second job in addition to his weekend gig at the theater. He was also a waiter at a café that his grandfather owned. He would rather have been a full-time projectionist, but his parents had always told him that family had to come first, and he really did adore his grandfather. The café was about seven or eight blocks away on the same street as the theater.

Marijke rushed directly over there. She went in the door, didn't ask to be seated, and dashed over to where Gustav was taking the orders of two elderly ladies.

"I've got to talk to you," she hissed.

"Not now, not now," Gustav replied. "Can't you see I'm taking an order?"

"It's urgent," Marijke said, raising her voice.

"Let me take this order first," Gustav insisted.

"Those people you work for on the weekends, at the movie theater down the street? They're hiding *Joden* in there! You've got to listen! You keep on working there, who knows? You could get caught up in it without even realizing it! Arrested, even!"

Maybe Marijke hadn't meant for her voice to carry. But it did.

A member of the NSB, the Dutch Nazi Party, was seated at a table with his loving pro-Nazi wife.

They both heard it.

So did the rest of the diners and staff at the restaurant.

———— ◉ ————

HENK AND KEES WERE ready to get moving.

They wished Bram would allow them to make their own way over to the old apartment. It wasn't like they didn't know the way to their own former home.

But Bram was adamant that they wait for him. "Look, if you wait until the end of the movie, it's going to be dark outside. There's less of a risk of anyone seeing you and recognizing you. We have to be strategic about this."

They knew he was right, yet they were anxious to get going.

Meanwhile, the movie still hadn't started yet.

It was maddening.

And about to get worse.

———— ◉ ————

NIKOLAAS COULDN'T BELIEVE it. The drama surrounding those Spranger children just kept on continuing non-stop.

He liked what his mother and father were doing for them, of course, yet at the same time, he hated it, too. Didn't they realize what a risk they were taking? Well, of course they did, but didn't they know how serious it might get if they were *caught*?

And they kept involving *him* too. Buying the bookstore and the apartment from Julius, giving both of those to him, temporarily of course, asking him to bring clothes and other articles for the children from the apartment, all of that hadn't been too much, but their latest idea was crazy. Totally. Completely. Insane.

Now they wanted to stash Kees, Henk and Rika with *him*.

His parents should take them home to their own place, but no. They were afraid Emmi might tell someone if they were stashed there.

At least, that night, his parents would be in his apartment, and he would be in theirs, basically babysitting for Emmi. Once there, he wouldn't be able to go home until the morning. Curfew nonsense.

He wasn't certain if he wanted to go back to his place anyway. What would he do in the apartment once it had been taken over by three *kinderen*?

The very idea didn't strike him as safe. The Nazis had been rounding up Jews every chance they got, and now he was supposed to host three of them?

Nikolaas wasn't a mean young man. He didn't think what the Nazis were doing was correct, or useful, as some of the antisemitic types proclaimed, and it certainly could never, ever qualify as decent. It was an abomination. He thought the Nazis were behaving worse than the barbarians of old in the way they kept hassling the Jews and sending them away, as if they weren't good enough to live in the country.

And this wasn't even the Nazis' own country in the first place! Oh, no, they didn't belong here, they'd *invaded* it, and they were enacting all of these laws and measures against the *Dutch* Jews!

This was definitely a major problem for the Netherlands. The country he loved, the one that still existed underneath the ugly red, white and black Nazi flag and the Gestapo and the marching soldiers who paraded in the streets.

It wasn't his problem to solve, though.

It wasn't his parents', either. They had to stop this set of circumstances as quickly as they could.

The sooner they could arrange for those Sprangers to hide someplace else, though, the better.

He closed up the book shop for the day and made his way over to the movie theater.

———————— ◉ ————————

PAOLO HAD BEEN MULLING over the questions that Emmi had asked.

The brats from next door thought the Van Der Graafs were hiding people in here.

He knew who those girls were, the ones with the mother who was living like an unpaid prostitute. Paolo wasn't a fan of that particular trade or anything, but he thought, at least, if a lady of the evening was selling herself for money, that it made a lot more sense than rutting like a rabbit with half the men in Amsterdam and giving it away for free. He could only speculate as to the upbringing that woman was giving her girls.

Even so, how in the world had the girls come up with such an accusation about the Van Der Graafs?

On the other hand, there were a few abnormalities that he had been noticing at work for some time.

That closed-up dressing room, for example. It was kept locked, but there were times when Paolo had been in the backstage area, and he'd heard a sound or two coming from in there. Nothing major. Just a light thump or, one memorable moment, what he had been sure was a cough.

It had made him jump out of his skin.

But then he immediately remembered that this was not a time to wonder too much about anything that was none of his business, or to ask too many questions. The Dutch Resistance had people all over the place, working behind the scenes to help defeat the Nazis. The Queen of the Netherlands herself had been on Radio Oranje, encouraging the Resistance.

A lot of folks were also displaced for one reason or another. It was entirely possible that God only knew who might currently be stashed in that room.

Yes.

It was possible.

Paolo suddenly didn't like the idea of working at the theater any longer.

———— ◉ ————

BRAM'S INSTRUCTIONS to Nikolaas had been to arrive at the theater right before the movie ended and to take his overly inquisitive pest of a little sister away from there as quickly as possible.

He found her by the refreshment counter. Bram had asked the old ticket taker, Gerritt, to cover it while Charlotta was out spiriting Rika away to Nik's apartment.

This was all so wild.

Emmi was reluctant to go with her brother, believing something was up, but he insisted. "We've got enough time to stop for ice cream," he told her. "And I'm hungry. Come on. Let's go."

Gerritt heard what they were saying.

"Have fun there, Emmi," he said to the little girl, who looked unusually cross.

Emmi had stored her coat and schoolbook satchel under the refreshment counter. She retrieved them.

Off they went.

They missed the arrival of the Green Police, the Nazis' cops, by only ten short minutes.

Chapter Fourteen

November 1942
Amsterdam, Netherlands

The movie let out.

Unfortunately, Bram was delayed a few minutes in retrieving the boys. An older customer had twisted an ankle coming down the balcony stairs and was literally moaning over it. Bram stayed with him until he could stand up and walk.

It only took maybe five minutes, but they were some of the longest ones of Bram's life.

He was moving across the auditorium to get to the dressing room at a fast pace, but he never got there.

That was when he heard it.

No, not it.

Them.

There were people coming in through the back door. The one that opened into the courtyard.

Several people.

Storming through that door, from the sound of them.

One of them was barking orders.

In German.

Bram took a deep breath.

He could have done an about-face. Turned right around, gone back through the auditorium, and tried to leave the theater out the front door, or by way of one of the fire exits, and gone into the street, but would that solve anything? He was the owner. He would be tracked down and held responsible no matter what he did.

If they caught him, maybe, at least, they wouldn't go after Charlotta, too.

So he went into the backstage area.

"Put your hands up!" A member of the Green Police ordered him in German, and then, for good measure, repeated it in Dutch.

Bram sighed and complied.

They had already broken down the door to the dressing room. The boys emerged, hands in the air. They looked scared.

All three soon found themselves taken away in the back of a truck, accompanied by three police guards.

And the only thing Bram could think of, during the ride to the prison, was why hadn't he let the boys go to the apartment when they had wanted to leave? If only. They wouldn't have been found there when the Green Police showed up, and all would still be well.

Now it wasn't.

In all probability, it might never be again.

———◦———

OLD GERRITT, BETJE and Paolo were the only ones still in the theater, the jolly weekday projectionist, Bartol, having already slipped out right behind the audience. Bram usually locked up, but he had been seized.

The cops questioned all three of the remaining theater employees.

Gerritt genuinely had not known what the hell was going on at the back of the theater and he said so. "I work here, out front," he said, indicating the ticket-taking stand.

Betje rarely left the box office while at work, so she said she was clueless about the situation at the rear of the building as well.

Paolo, thanks to Emmi, actually did have some idea of what had been going on, but he quickly decided that since he wasn't absolutely one hundred percent sure if the rumor the child had relayed to him was true, he was going to act as though he'd never heard it. After all, he had no proof anyone had been concealed in the building. A thump here, a cough behind a locked door there, none of it added up to anything like solid evidence, he told himself.

He was feeding himself a lie, and knew it. Thumps and especially coughs coming from a locked room that was supposedly empty could lead to only one conclusion, and that was that there was someone there behind the door. But the Nazis didn't have to know Paolo realized that. He would pretend he didn't know a thing.

The two remaining agents questioned the trio of employees, but it didn't get them anywhere. They emphatically stated they weren't in on it.

"We just work here," Gerritt finally said, a little desperately, since he was worried he'd be taken into custody for something he genuinely didn't do.

The arrested owner, now, he was the one who had hidden the boys, and the Nazi cops already had heard it. The tipoff they'd gotten earlier that afternoon had been given by someone who said so specifically. "Go after the owner, Bram Van Der Graaf," the voice of the caller had said before hanging up. They were also planning to question his wife.

"This theater is closed until further notice," the thinner of the two Green Policemen, the one who had taken the informer's call, told Betje, Paolo and Gerritt. "Do any of you have the keys to lock it up?"

"I do," said Gerritt.

"All right. You three can go, though we might come back with more questions for you at some point. Lock up the place first," the agent said, like he had the right to issue an imperial order, and with that, he and his crony left.

The Green Police had an interesting evening planned. They'd be interrogating Bram, Henk, Kees.

"I wonder," said Paolo after they left, "who in the world was hidden here. Who they found."

"I," Betje decided and announced out loud, "am not going to ask anybody around here *any* questions."

———◦———

THE ICE CREAM PARLOR was a block from the theater. Gerritt always passed it on his way to go home and saw through the window that Emmi and Nikolaas were inside, seated at a little table and eating sundaes.

He went in.

He had no desire for an ice cream cone or a sundae. Who could even think of having such a treat, after what had just happened?

Bram arrested! And for doing something good, too.

But Nikolaas didn't know about it yet, and needed to be told. Gerritt had to tell him. To warn him. The Green Police had found something they considered "wrong" going on, and closed the theater, so more official scrutiny was no doubt on the way for the Van Der Graafs.

"Gerritt! Come and join us," Emmi smiled. She waved him over to their table.

He didn't need to be asked there twice. "Emmi, my girl. Could you do an old man with bad legs a favor, go stand on line, and order me an ice cream cone?" He handed her enough coins to cover it.

"Of course!" Emmi took the money and headed for the counter. That put her out of earshot.

Gerritt settled in a chair and said to Nikolaas in a low voice, "I didn't want to speak in front of her. Nikolaas, there's trouble. There was a raid at the theater. Just now. Something or other about hidden Jews. Who knows? Your father was taken."

"He was *what?*" Nikolaas asked in a whisper, jerking back in his chair as if he'd just been shot in the heart.

Gerritt nodded. "Yes. I'm afraid so. They took your father away, arrested. Closed the theater until further notice, too."

"I can't believe this," Nikolaas breathed, but that wasn't exactly the case. He could. He had been afraid of something like this all along, and here it was.

"I don't know who else they may have taken because I didn't see it. Apparently the Green Police raided from the back of the theater, from the courtyard door. They were asking Paolo, Betje and me about hidden people, so if there were any of those in there, they must have nabbed them too. I knew nothing about it." He added, "Nikolaas, I'm so sorry to be the one to tell you. But you need to be extra careful right now since they'll probably be coming back with more questions."

"And my mother?" Nikolaas asked Gerritt, dreading to hear his answer.

"She left early. I was running the refreshment stand for her."

That was enough to make Nikolaas breathe a sigh of relief. His mother got out of there. This probably, hopefully, meant that so did Rika. That had been the plan.

Gerritt gestured toward where Emmi was still waiting in line at the counter. "I don't know what you should, or shouldn't, say to her. They're sure to return and aren't above asking children questions."

"I'll tell her nothing at all while we're in here, at least," Nikolaas said. The last thing he needed on his hands was for his little sister to cause a scene in public. It would only run the risk of more attention being focused on his family. "And as little as possible later. I don't know what to do beyond that," he added.

Gerritt looked at the distraught young man and sized him up. He had known the Van Der Graaf family for so many years. Bram's late father had been the first owner of the theater, and they had been fast friends. Nikolaas was a good sort, always had been, if slightly lacking in courage at times, and he didn't deserve to find himself in the middle of this current horrific situation. Bram under arrest. Jews having to hide so they wouldn't be deported from their own country. People being concealed in the movie theater. You couldn't make these kinds of developments up.

Gerritt came to a decision at that moment. "I know of someone," he told Nikolaas, his voice hardly above a whisper, "who might be, let's just say, *useful* to you."

"I'm all ears," Nikolaas replied, also *sotto voce*.

"Name is Lovisa. She tends the bar at Maartje's Restaurant near the Rijksmuseum. Tell her Gerritt sent you and can vouch for you." He didn't add that Lovisa was his niece, and as trustworthy as a person could be in times like these. "A true patriot," he said instead.

Lovisa, Nikolaas repeated to himself. Maartje's. The Rijksmuseum. She must be in the Resistance.

"Got it," he nodded.

The sooner he went to see Lovisa, he thought, the better.

"SLIGHT CHANGE OF PLAN," Nikolaas told his little sister in as casual a tone as he could manage once they said good night to Gerritt and left the ice cream shop. He couldn't bring her home to Charlotta and Bram's apartment if there was any chance that the Gestapo or the Green Police might show up to interrogate his mother there, to see if she was involved, and he wasn't going to take her to his own place, either, where, presumably, Rika was now in hiding. All he could do at the moment was make sure Emmi was kept totally out of the fray. "I'm going to drop you off at Mevrouw Brink's place."

"Mevrouw Brink!" Emmi exclaimed. Mevrouw Brink had been her second-grade teacher. She still worked at Emmi's school and had become a very close friend of the family. Emmi loved spending time with her.

But this was suspicious. "I'd like that. But why?" She asked her brother now as they walked along the busy darkening street. An icy wind was blowing from a northerly direction. The child shivered.

"Because I've heard there's rumors of trouble tonight," he answered her vaguely, making it up as he went along. "Roundups of men." It was as good a lie as any. Men were always at risk of being grabbed and sent to Germany. "I don't want you walking around with me, Emmi, it isn't safe tonight." As if it was on any night. "Annabel Brink lives close to your school, and her place is right around the corner from here. I want to stash you there for the evening. You can go to school with her tomorrow."

"In the same dress as I'm wearing today?" Emmi wailed.

Girls and their outfits, Nikolaas almost groaned. "You'll survive that."

"I'm being made fun of enough already," Emmi told him. Now it was her turn to lower her voice. "Neeltje and Lena Teemink were saying my parents hide Jews."

That stopped Nikolaas in his tracks. "They said *what?*"

His little sis nodded. "Yes. They said that, and then at recess they and two more kids started chasing me around and yelling it. It was awful."

"I can just bet it was," Nikolaas agreed. He was furious. Furious! The Teemink girls were the daughter of the harlot who lived next door to the theater, that wretched Corina. The mother, if you could call her that, not only came on to Bram on a regular basis but to Nik as well. She had tried to seduce him when he was thirteen years old. Those Temminks were quite a family, and he didn't mean that in the best of directions, either.

Living next door to the theater.

Had they heard something coming from behind the blackout curtains over the dressing room window?

Noticed anything strange?

Oh, God.

They must have.

How else might they have known?

Chapter Fifteen

November 1942
Amsterdam, Netherlands

RIKA CAME OUT OF HER long, lovely soak in the bathtub ready to stay up until her brothers and Bram arrived, but then she had another idea. She was going to lie down in her own bed for a few minutes, or so she thought.

Two hours later she was still fast asleep while Charlotta fretted over a cup of imitation coffee in the dining room, becoming more frantic by the second.

There was still no sign of the boys and Bram. They should have arrived an hour and a half earlier!

Finally, just minutes before curfew, Nikolaas showed up, and this wasn't part of the plan. He was supposed to go to her apartment with Emmi, not here to his place, and Emmi, horror of horrors, wasn't with him.

"What's going on?" She asked him anxiously, but in the usual wartime whisper, afraid the walls had ears, as she pulled him in through the door.

Her son sat down on one of the dining room chairs, Charlotta in another one beside him. "Where's Rika?" He asked first.

"Sound asleep in her old room. Nikolaas, what happened? Why are you here? And where's Emmi?" Charlotta almost choked with fright on saying her daughter's name.

"Mevrouw Brink's," he replied. "I wanted to get her out of the way tonight. Mama, there's no easy way to say this. Papa got arrested.

The Green Police knew about the boys, raided the theater through the courtyard door, and I am pretty sure they found them, although I wasn't there when it happened. I heard about it secondhand from Gerritt." He put his elbows on the table, his head in his hands, and added angrily, "I believe those awful Temminks betrayed us."

He went into the whole story.

"Oh," Charlotta faltered when he was finished. "Oh, *no*."

"I could kill those Temminks," her son raged.

"If it was them, then I would help you. Though how can we know for certain? It might not have been them, either. Remember what happened last night? That drunk Hannus Douw sleeping it off in the theater? It could have been him. Your father was afraid he'd report us. Maybe he did."

"What a choice of betrayers. A whore and a drunk," Nikolaas fumed. "The thing is, we don't know if this Douw character reported us, but we do know the Temmink girls were screaming it in Emmi's face all over the schoolyard. Emmi told me. They've probably already spread it all over town. And if they have, anybody could have reported us for it."

"There's rewards," Charlotta replied dully. "For turning in hidden Jews. The Nazis pay people for that."

"I wouldn't put it past Corina Temmink to want to cause us a heap of trouble and get her hands on some Reichsmarks in the bargain. She would probably love to *pak de poen*." Grab the money.

"As if she doesn't have access to enough of it already," his mother sighed, "having inherited her decent husband's jewelry shop. Was he ever bamboozled by that woman! He died defending Holland, a hero, and there she is, sleeping around, and liable to do anything, including reporting hidden Dutch Jewish *children* to the enemy. If she really was the one who did it."

"I'd bet on her over Douw," Nik ventured, "though who really knows? I didn't meet Douw."

"How in the world," asked Charlotta, who still hadn't been fully hit yet by the bad news about Bram, "are we going to break this news to Rika?" She thought it was important to concentrate, first and foremost, right then, on the one Spranger child they had left.

"For now, let her sleep, Ma. Meanwhile, we've got to find a way to get her out of here. I have a lead," he added, thinking of this Lovisa that Gerritt recommended, "and will follow it up tomorrow."

"No you won't," Charlotta told him. "You pass that lead on to me. I'll be the one to go after it. You've done enough. I want you out of all this from this point on."

So he told her of Gerritt's suggestion that they contact Lovisa, the bartender at Maartje's Restaurant, and where it was located.

"Maybe you need to go someplace else until it's all over, too," Charlotta said wearily. "They keep taking Dutch men away to work in Germany, and I *do not* want you going there." She added fiercely, "I won't lose anyone else."

ANNABEL BRINK HAD BEEN horrified, earlier in the day, when word went circulating around the teachers' room about what the Temmink brats had been saying to taunt little Emmi Van Der Graaf.

"I stopped them," said the teacher who had pulled Emmi away from the others at recess, "but it couldn't be a worse accusation. They were accusing the child of coming from a family that is harboring *onderduikers!*"

Onderduikers literally meant "under divers," like submarines. It was the current popular word used to describe those in hiding.

"That's dangerous," Mevrouw Brink had said.

"Of course it is," said another teacher. "I seriously have to wonder about those Temminks. The mother's a disaster area and look at the two of those girls. Not even enough sense *not* to make such a claim, and probably without an ounce of proof, either. Just pure meanness."

That had been the conversation at lunchtime. Mevrouw Brink was shocked to the core when Nikolaas Van Der Graaf came, out of the blue, and delivered Emmi to her doorstep later that same day.

All he said was, "Can my sister stay here tonight?"

Annabel Brink had answered, "But of course," and ushered the child into her parlor.

Nikolaas offered no explanations.

"Stay safe," Annabel Brink had urged the girl's older brother as he went on his way.

Emmi didn't seem to have a clue as to what was going on, but once her brother had left, she confided that she thought there was some kind of a problem.

That was all she said. If there was any truth to the accusation made by Neeltje and Lena Temmink about her parents, she didn't want to dare mentioning it to anyone else besides Paolo. Not even one of her favorite people like Mevrouw Brink.

———◉———

LOVISA JANSEN IMMEDIATELY recognized the lovely woman who entered Maartje's the next afternoon. It was Charlotta, the wife of the owner of the theater where her Uncle Gerritt had worked for most of his life.

"How can I help you?" She asked Charlotta in a welcoming tone of voice.

"Are you Lovisa?"

"I certainly am," the bartender smiled.

"I could use a few drops of wine, if you have it," Charlotta replied. Then she turned the palm of her hand in Lovisa's direction. It held a tiny scrap of paper for the woman to see. "Gerritt sent me," she had written on it. The code phrase Nikolaas had passed along to her.

Lovisa nodded almost imperceptibly. "Of course we have wine. No shortage of that today. Just give me a moment," she told her. "If you're alone, why don't you have a seat at that table for two over there?"

"I will," Charlotta replied. She settled herself at the table and took in the décor of the restaurant. It was lovely, calm. Bright walls, wooden furniture, and with an Art Nouveaux design. It felt like she had just gone back to another, happier time period, one before all the current craziness started.

Lovisa came back with a crystal wine glass filled with a golden liquid and a newspaper, the *Deutsche Zeitung*. It was a German paper, and filled with propaganda, but Charlotta could hardly refuse it in a public space filled with patrons of unknown persuasions. "Here's your drink, madam. Someone left this paper here. I thought you might enjoy having a look at it." She gave Charlotta a pointed look.

Something I need to see is inside of this paper, she realized.

"Dirk the waiter will be by momentarily to take your order," Lovisa added, and moved along, back to her spot behind the bar.

Charlotta began looking at the paper. The date, today's date, had been underlined in pencil.

She found what else she sought on the third page.

It was written in pencil at the very bottom.

An address.

Located in the "De Pijp" neighborhood. The part of the city known as Amsterdam-Zuid, the Old South area.

And a time, written as "1700."

17:00, in other words.

Today.

Five o'clock at night.

ALONE THAT SAME AFTERNOON, and still back in her old apartment, Rika was a crying mess of misery, combined with a bad case of shattered nerves.

How could it have happened the way it did?

Why were her brothers taken, yesterday of all days, just as they were almost free of the theater, the way she had been?

Obviously there had been an informant, but who was it? For the most part, the three of them had been so careful the entire time they were hidden there. Weren't they?

Had that awful drunk of a man who had been in the theater and discovered them caused this disaster to happen?

I will find him after the war, she vowed, and I'll make him wish he'd never been born, if it turns out to be him.

Furthermore, Bram, who had been so valiant in his efforts at protecting them, was gone, too. Charlotta was at risk just for being his wife and Nikolaas could face Nazi scrutiny because he was the grown son.

It was horrendous.

This apartment had once been her family's, but now she could not wait to get out of there.

———⊙———

THAT EVENING CHARLOTTA went to the address she had memorized from the note in the German newspaper before she gave it back to Lovisa while still in the restaurant.

It turned out to be a Catholic church, three blocks in from the Amstelkanaal.

The door was open, so she went inside and sat down in one of the pews toward the back. By that point it was already dark outside so no light shone through the stained-glass windows. The nave was dimly lighted, but lit, up front, by several long candle tapers.

There was a priest up on the altar, straightening a cloth over the altar table. He went away for a moment and then returned with a vase of flowers that he put in front of the table.

She saw only two other people there at that hour. One lady was utilizing the kneeling bench while she prayed silently. That looked like a good idea, so Charlotta knelt on one and folded her hands in prayer, too.

She was not a particularly religious woman but on that day of all days she didn't have to go through the motions of praying. Charlotta actually knelt there and prayed for real. "Get us through this, please, God," she begged the Almighty. "Get my family and the children of my friends through this atrocious war. We need to live to see the other side."

At that point, someone sat in the pew behind her and cleared her throat.

Charlotta turned.

And there, she found Lovisa.

BRAM HAD BEEN SEPARATED from the boys, and the boys were not kept in a cell with each other.

It was their second day of relentless questioning. The Green Police put all of them through a whole battery of questions. How long had they been in hiding? Who helped besides Bram? Who knew? Who else was hidden?

These three were driving the main interrogator berserk. The two boys would only say that Bram was involved. That was it. Just Bram.

No mention of Charlotta.

Not a word about the help they'd received from Nikolaas.

They also did not mention Rika at all. Not one word about the sister they hoped had gotten away.

Bram did the same. He didn't give up one single word about Charlotta, Nikolaas, or Rika.

What the Nazis didn't know what that their silence had been decided upon before they'd even been put onto the truck that took them to the jail. There had been a moment when the men who had raided the dressing room were so busy talking to one another that they had all but ignored Bram, Henk and Kees.

"Total silence," Bram had whispered. "About the others. None of us should reveal a thing."

"We wouldn't," Kees had said, "and you know it."

And that was that.

No way were they going to help the Nazis arrest more people, especially Rika, Charlotta, and Nikolaas.

They were, all three, already trapped in a no-win situation, and they knew it.

They were going to stick to the plan.

———————⊙———————

ONCE LOVISA HEARD CHARLOTTA'S whispered story she said there wasn't a moment left to waste.

"We should move the girl, and your son, tomorrow," she said. "Send them to Maartje's Restaurant, very early. Can you get them there by six-thirty in the morning, before it opens?"

"I think so," nodded Charlotta.

"Make sure so. I will ask them, 'How is Tante Lini?' And the response to that is, 'Much improved.' No luggage, no suitcases, nothing obvious that would mark them as being on the move. We can get them whatever they need later. I can arrange transportation to a temporary hideout for each of them, where we can get them some new identification papers, and from there, they can go on to someplace even better."

"They'll be there," Charlotta promised. "At Maartje's."

"Just the two of them, ma'am. Not you. You should come back to the restaurant the day after tomorrow, in the afternoon, and I will give you an indication of how it went. Not out loud and directly, of course. But in a way so you'll know."

"I understand," said Charlotta. Then, thinking of her earlier message in the German newspaper, she added, "You're quite good at that sort of thing."

It made Lovisa smile.

"Remember," she said. "Tante Lini. Much improved."

After that exchange, Lovisa said she would leave the church in ten more minutes. She suggested that Charlotta be on her way, and proceeded up the aisle, toward the candles that people lit as an accompaniment to their prayers, which were to the side of the altar.

Lovisa could have easily passed for the living embodiment of holiness and spirituality.

No one would think by looking at her that she was actually there as an underground Dutch Resistance operative.

Chapter Sixteen

November 1942
The Netherlands

———◦———

CHARLOTTA WASN'T BACK outside the church, and walking along the dark November streets, before she had to ask herself just what in the world was she *doing?* She had met Lovisa only that afternoon, and now she was going to entrust her beloved son and her friends' daughter to her?

Yet what else could she do? She had no other contacts in the branch of the Resistance that resettled endangered people. Gerritt trusted this girl, he'd recommended they contact her, and he'd always been a rock. But what if he was wrong about her?

She'd have to trust Lovisa. There really wasn't any other choice.

Of course, if Gerritt was less than what he appeared, Lovisa could be, too.

Charlotta chided herself for such a thought. The raid was suddenly making her suspicious of *everybody*.

Gerritt had been reliable during the over two decades she had known him. It would be all right.

At least, that's what she hoped.

It was Lovisa or nothing.

———◦———

EMMI HAD BEEN SITTING in the hallway in front of her apartment door for more than two hours.

No one was home. Not her mother and not her father, either.

She had gone, first, to the theater after school, just the way she always did, only to find there was a sign on the front doors proclaiming it was TEMPORARILY CLOSED.

Closed? She'd had no warning about *that*.

She was hungry, thirsty, and had to use the bathroom. What was happening with her crazy family *now?* If she had wondered before, now she wished she had the power to demand the answer out of her parents at once.

That was if they hadn't been rounded up or were already among those who had disappeared. The child was getting all filled up with dread by pondering the menace of the Nazi regime. And dread or no dread, the theater was shuttered, her parents weren't home, and she was locked out.

What should I do? She asked herself. My mother and father seem to have forgotten me. Either that or they're gone for good. Should I go back to Mevrouw Brink's place?

A neighbor woman, Henrietta Blazer, finally came along before either of her parents did. "Emmi, my dear, you look miserable. Are you locked out?"

Emmi didn't want to cry. "Yes." And that was just for starters.

"Come with me to my place, then. We can listen to the radio until your parents get home."

Mevrouw Blazer reached out a hand to Emmi and pulled her up off the floor. They went into her apartment. It was right next door to the Van Der Graaf's.

Henrietta was a widow who loved flowers and had the place decorated with a lot of silk ones in vases. For the moment Emmi, who normally loved looking around the place, didn't even care. "Can I use the water closet?"

"Of course, child, go ahead."

Once she was done in there, Henrietta called out for Emmi to join her in the kitchen. "I have a stash of cocoa powder in here that I've been keeping for a special occasion," she told the child. "I think your visit calls for one. Can I make you a hot chocolate?"

A slow smile spread across the little girl's face. "I'd like that."

———◉———

CHARLOTTA REALLY HAD forgotten about Emmi for the moment.

She made it back to Nikolaas' apartment with forty-five minutes to spare before the curfew went into effect.

It only took her a minute or two to relay the instructions from Lovisa to her son and Rika. "No suitcases or satchels. Take nothing obvious along with you or it will look like you're about to flee. You know the drill. Get to Maartje's Restaurant near the Rijksmuseum at six-thirty tomorrow morning. Wait outside for Lovisa to show up. She'll ask you, 'How is your Tante Lini?' And your response should be, 'Much improved.' After that, Lovisa will take it from there."

"That's it?" Nikolaas asked

"That's it. Gerritt trusts Lovisa so you should, too."

That was when she finally remembered she had an elementary school-age daughter who was probably waiting to get into their locked apartment at home. "Oh my God! *Emmi!* I have to get home to her. Right now. Just be there at Maartje's tomorrow, okay? Courage!"

And off Charlotta went.

———◉———

SO ALL I CAN TAKE ALONG this time is my purse, Rika thought.

She still had her mother's jewelry that she'd grabbed the first time she had to flee in there. There hadn't been much of a reason to open her purse again once she was hidden in the theater. Oh, well.

Now she took the family jewels out. She went into her parents' old room, the one Nikolaas now occupied, and found a few more valuable pieces, rubies and diamonds and emeralds. It wouldn't hurt to have them.

Rummaging around through her mother's dresser drawers, she managed to find a zippered cosmetic bag. Perfect. She also took one of her mother's lace handkerchiefs and wrapped the jewelry in that before hiding it in the bag.

There was money hidden under a book in one of her mother's drawers, too. Rika was about to take it but then remembered. It was in Dutch guilders, and the Nazis had banned them, replacing the currency with Reichsmarks.

A shame. Wherever she was going, those guilders might have come in handy if they were still legal currency. But it was like so much else that went on these days. They weren't, and that was that.

She found a new toothbrush, still in its wrapper, in the bathroom cabinet and grabbed that, along with a small tube of toothpaste. Those she wrapped in a washcloth. If she had to take "half a baths" again wherever she was going, she wanted to do so with a washcloth from home. From her room she took a comb for her hair.

It would have been nice to grab some soap and shampoo, but her purse was already bulging with stuff by then, and what if she was stopped? How could she explain having a bottle of shampoo in her purse? Hopefully she'd be able to get her hands on some wherever she was going to be.

That was it. All she had left to do was figure out what dress, vest, sweater and coat to wear when she left in the morning.

———— ◉ ————

HENRIETTA BLAZER AND Emmi sipped their hot chocolate while listening to the Dutch news broadcast from England that went out over the BBC.

Or, at least, Henrietta listened to it. Emmi was too distracted to follow it along. She was warmed by the hot chocolate, but her brain couldn't handle much else.

Finally, miraculously, she thought she heard a key entering the lock in the door across the hallway.

Her doorway!

"I think they're home," she exclaimed, jumping up from her place at Henrietta's table to fling open the door.

And there was Charlotta, struggling to get in.

"Mama!" Emmi all but cheered.

"Oh, thank God! Thank God, thank God, thank God," Charlotta exalted. "Emmi!" She ran to her child and hugged her tight. "My poor darling, this has been such a day, I simply wasn't able to get home any sooner."

"So long as you're home now, it's okay," Emmi replied.

"What happened?" Henrietta Blazer asked Charlotta. "Were you caught up in another one of those dreadful *razzias?*" She meant a street raid where the Nazis rounded up people to send to Germany, mostly Jews. The Nazis often checked everyone's identity cards, usually keeping the Jews and letting the non-Jews go, although some days they took them, too.

"Nothing that wretched," Charlotta replied, evading telling her neighbor the truth. What could she say? Excuse me, but I went to two separate rendez-vous to meet up with a member of the Resistance who will be smuggling my son and the daughter of Jewish friends out of Amsterdam tomorrow?

It couldn't be spoken out loud.

Just the same, Charlotta, who had always, at least before the war, prided herself on being an honest and forthright woman, was becoming fairly tired of being put in one position after another where it was imperative for her to lie, tell half-truths, leave things out, or make things up. It may have been a necessity at the moment, but it never felt right.

"Thank you so much for taking care of Emmi for me," Charlotta said instead of elaborating, thus changing the subject.

"She should feel free knock on my door if this ever happens again," Henrietta Blazer said. "These days just about anything is possible. Anything bad. I found her in the hallway, looking like an orphan and trying not to cry."

That was almost enough to break Charlotta's heart in two, although she tried her best not to show it. "I'm hoping it won't happen again. Thank you, Henrietta. Come on, Emmi."

The girl ran back to the table first, finished the rest of her hot cocoa in one fast gulp, and was ready to go home with her mother. It was too rare a treat to abandon.

The first thing she said when they got inside the door was, "Where's Father?"

It was the question Charlotta was dreading. How to explain this? "Darling, you'd better sit down."

Charlotta didn't think it was a good idea to tell the girl that her father had been arrested for hiding Jews. Right from the beginning, she and Bram had felt that the less Emmi knew, the better. A secret this big was enough of a burden for the adults. How much worse might it be for a child to have to keep it?

Yet those Temmink girls had revealed it before Charlotta had even had a chance to tell Emmi directly.

Still and all, she did not want to let her child know that Neeltje and Lena Temmink had gotten it right. She'd be better off believing they had the entire tale all wrong. Once the war was finally over, then, Charlotta promised herself, she would set Emmi straight about everything.

"Your father," she explained, "was caught in a raid."

That, at least, was a half-truth.

Chapter Seventeen

November 1942
The Netherlands

———◉———

IT SEEMED TO RIKA LIKE the month of November was never going to end.

The next morning, she and Nikolaas were up at five, dressed, ready, and out the door on the very stroke of six o'clock. It was time to meet this Lovisa gal at Maartje's Restaurant near the Rijksmuseum, which was about a half an hour's walk away.

Rika was pleased all over again, almost joyous, even, to find herself out on the street. All those months hiding in the dark of the theater like a little tulip bulb beneath the surface had given her a whole new appreciation for the great outdoors.

Yet the young girl's mind was forever searching for glitches, problems and pitfalls these days, and she zeroed in on a big one. Her father had been arrested while trying to get fake identity cards for the family. Months ago, Bram had taken her actual card away and burned it because it had her listed as a Jew.

Not having an identity card, no matter what a person's religion happened to be, was yet another of the many stupid reasons the Nazis could have you arrested.

Of course, if they weren't stopped and asked for one, then it wouldn't be a problem. But if they were, more trouble.

They were in luck that day. No patrols crossed their paths.

Once they got to the restaurant, they waited a little uncertainly by the front entrance for Lovisa.

"We should have asked my mother what she looks like, this Lovisa," Nikolaas commented to Rika. "We don't even know."

"Typically Dutch, I'd be willing to bet," Rika replied. "Blonde hair, blue eyes."

"And wearing a Dutch national costume too?" He teased. "With an apron and a lace hat?"

"If she has one, she's probably saving it to wear until the end of the war," Rika replied.

When Lovisa did arrive, she turned out to be a lovely yet remote brunette in a stylish green coat. Green eyes, too. The color of the coat enhanced them which may have been the reason why she picked it out in the first place. Very pretty, Nikolaas thought.

"Well, hello there, *cousins,*" she greeted them with enthusiasm. "How is Tante Lini?"

Nikolaas replied, "Much improved!"

"Good old Aunt Lini," Rika got into the spirit of the charade and added with a smile.

"That's what I was hoping you'd tell me. This way," she directed the two of them with an efficient little nod, and they followed her away from the restaurant.

"We're only going three more blocks," she added softly as they moved along. "Destination is the Amstelkanaal. And by the way," she added under her breath, "it's a pleasure to meet you both."

"Same here," smiled Nikolaas. He was already smitten with the woman. She looked to be in her mid-twenties, just like him. He hoped that the walk with her would never end, but all too soon, it did.

Once they reached the water she directed them to a long, flat-topped canal boat. "This is the one. It's going to be making milk deliveries this morning. You're to ride along in the hold. You'll each be dropped off where you need to go."

A man who was in the prow of the boat smiled as if he had known them their entire lives instead of only meeting the duo just that minute. "There you are! Come in and join me," he urged.

Nikolaas and Rika were happy to oblige.

The man didn't give them his name, and he didn't ask for theirs, either. They settled on wooden crates inside of the hold that were right by a window. It was covered by two layers of curtains, some kind of netting in front of the usual ugly blackout type.

"I wish I could open that and take a look at everything," Rika sighed.

The jolly boat pilot told her it would be all right if she peeked out of the edge of it.

"Just don't pull it open completely," he added. "You don't want anyone knowing this vessel is carrying a more precious cargo than, ah, milk."

That gave Rika a warm feeling.

The morning could not have been nicer. It was cold out, but sunny. The northern sky was a robin's egg blue streaked with long white clouds, and it wasn't long before the barge turned from the canal and started sailing along the Amstel River. Houses, people, leafless trees, buildings, other boats, it was all so fabulous!

It was over an hour and a few stops later before the gentleman called Rika away from her post by the window. It was time, he said, for her to get off. They had reached one of the spots where he had to leave several crates of bottled milk. "Just wait on the bench there. It won't be long," he promised her.

"Goodbye," she said hesitantly to him and to Nikolaas. She watched rather sadly as the boat glided away. Nikolaas was her last contact with home, and he was being taken somewhere else.

Where was she? The backless bench where she sat down to wait was on a concrete dock behind a long building. It looked like she was sitting alone at the back of a warehouse. A *deserted* one, she assumed, from the unkempt look of the place and the number of weeds growing around it. There was nothing on the other side of the canal except for what appeared to be one small farmhouse. Other than that, there was nothing but empty fields.

Rika was uneasy at first. The wind picked up.

What town was this?

What was that building used for?

And why were there no people here to meet her and pick up the crates of milk?

———●———

CHARLOTTA KEPT EMMI home from school that day.

The girl had been wildly upset when she heard that Bram had been caught in a Nazi trap and she hadn't even been told a fraction of it. Charlotta used the fact that she'd been up crying for most of the night as the reason to keep her home, but that wasn't it at all.

She didn't want her daughter returning to that school. Not when those Temmink girls, or, more than likely, their atrocious mother Corina, might have been the ones to betray Bram and the boys.

There had to be some other school for the child to attend. Even if Charlotta had to pay for her to go to a different one, she would do that to get her Emmi out of there.

She felt an urgency about this, a sense of the walls closing in on her if she didn't, and on Emmi, too.

If Corina had been the one who turned in Bram, she could turn in Charlotta, too.

This was a Friday. She wanted her daughter out of that school by Monday at the latest.

She had just brought Emmi back over to Henrietta Blazer's apartment, where she asked the neighbor to keep her, if she would, for the morning, and gone back inside, when two members of the Green Police, the occupier's cops, knocked on the door.

———●———

RIKA REMAINED ALONE on the bench.

The girl never, ever thought she would have a thought like the one that went through her head at that particular moment, but she suddenly missed her pitch-dark room back at the theater. It hadn't been much, she hadn't even had a real bed in there, or a chair, either, but it had felt a whole lot safer than this.

Were Lovisa and the boat pilot really as trustworthy as she had been led to believe?

On the bench, she seemed to be exposed here on all sides.

What to do about it?

And that warehouse! She looked at it uneasily again. That could only be an abandoned building. Rika was sure of it. Some of the windows were even broken.

Eerie.

Why had the boatman delivered crates of milk to a building where nobody worked?

Should she just sit here, wait and hope that somebody trustworthy would arrive to pick her up?

What if whoever came along and found her turned out *not* to be the right person? Some NSB-er could come along then where would she be?

Rika thought she could always run for it, but then, where could she go? This area seemed like the middle of nowhere. Really and truly, this was not good.

She would wait a few more minutes, but then, that was it. If nobody came, she'd have to make her way back to Amsterdam and get in touch with Charlotta, but she hated that idea. Charlotta had already given up enough for Rika. The theater was shuttered. Bram was apprehended. Her brothers were arrested. Who knew what else might happen?

Of course, if there wasn't any other choice, she would have to find her way back to Charlotta. From here, this desolate place, she wasn't even sure which direction she'd have to go to get there. And when would be a safe time to go? Not at night, with the curfew, or by day, without papers, and...

"Hallo," a voice suddenly called out from the direction to the right of the building.

Rika had been looking across the water at the field and the farmhouse, so she turned around.

"Hallo there," came the voice again.

It was coming from a teenage girl, cute as a pixie, one who looked to be about Rika's age. Her hair was worn in long blonde braids tied with blue ribbons.

When she reached Rika, she asked her, "How is Tante Lini?"

"She – she is much improved," Rika replied, stammering the reply out of the nervousness she had been feeling. The girl knew the code words! Oh, thank goodness! It seemed to be all right after all. She just hadn't expected such a young girl to be her contact.

"I'm so sorry to be late picking you up. Don't tell my parents, all right? They'll kill me. I was supposed to be here already, but wouldn't you know it? I overslept. Come on, then. Back this way."

Rika expected the girl to go towards the wretched building. She didn't. Instead, she showed her to a dirt path that followed the river through a copse of trees. Beyond the trees they came to a small brick house.

"We live here," the girl explained. "I'm Evy. But you know how it goes, don't you? No last names with *projects* like this. And you're Rosa."

"Rosa? No, Evy, my name is – "

"Don't tell me," the girl said. "We've already got someone who started making documentation for you. Your new name is going to be Rosa Van der Linden. Do you like it?"

"Rosa Van der Linden," Rika repeated. "Yes, I do!" The first name meant "rose," the last, "from the linden trees." Like a rose growing by linden trees! It was so pretty, and so magnificently Dutch. *Undisputedly* Dutch. "It's a *wonderful* name!"

"So glad you like it. I picked it out for you myself," Evy grinned, "when I heard you were my age. That's one of my jobs, helping to come up with new names for those who, you know, *visit us* for a little while."

Who hid with them temporarily, that's what Rika realized she meant.

"Come on," Evy added, "into the house we go. It's already pretty cold out here."

"But what about the milk back there?" Rika asked as they stepped through the door, thinking it would be a shame to let the crates of milk go bad if no one retrieved them. She'd heard there were increasing food shortages. "Nobody picked it up."

"Milk?" Evy looked puzzled. "Oh, you mean the containers that were dropped off? Those don't hold milk, silly. They're just labeled that way!" She laughed as if this was hilarious, but she didn't elaborate further.

Rika stepped inside the little house. Oil paintings decorated the light green painted walls, carpets were on the floor, and there were overstuffed chairs and a sofa with doilies on them.

Evy's mother called out, "Come join us in the kitchen for some nice, hot porridge."

And all at once, Rika felt like she had arrived at a house that was safe.

Chapter Eighteen

December 1942
Somewhere in the Netherlands

EVY'S FATHER WAS A doctor, her mother, a nurse. They had met years ago at the hospital where the two of them still worked, fell in love, married, and within a year had added plenty of sunshine to their lives by having a daughter like Evy.

"Doctors, nurses," the father told Rika that first morning at breakfast, "we're about helping people. I took an oath when I became a doctor that begins, 'First, do no harm.'"

"When the Nazis invaded," Evy put in, "it was obvious. That was the start of a whole *lot* of harm."

"Was it ever!" Agreed her mother. "So we've tried to do what we can to alleviate that, one person at a time."

Rika smiled. "Thank you so much for what you're doing for me."

"We need to take your photo for your new identification papers," the doctor told her. "Right after breakfast."

Evy added, "Rosa," with a grin.

Rika couldn't remember the last time she'd had as much fun with anybody as she did that wonderful week staying with this upbeat family. She had almost forgotten how to act her own age, but Evy was able to remind her. The bubbly girl would come home from school with hilarious tales of tyrannical teachers and cute boys and the girls who were her friends, not to mention a few others that she couldn't withstand. It was enough to make Rika wish she could enroll in that school, too.

The girls shared a room, played board games, talked of the clothes they'd buy after the war when the clothing shortages ended, and the food they'd eat, too.

And they discussed movies. Evy had seen a lot of the recent ones, and, from her hiding place, Rika had *heard* them, at least, over and over. They talked of movies long into the night just about every night, with Evy describing the scenes that Rika, of necessity, had missed seeing.

Evy showed her a false wall up in the attic, where Rika could hide if any strangers came by the isolated little house, but nobody did. The German police force, known as the "Green Police" from the color of their uniforms, as opposed to the "Black Police," who were Dutch, were known to make raids on houses, looking for Jews, as if they didn't have anything better to do, like arrest real criminals. They didn't raid this one. Rika remained, during the day, in Evy's room, behind the protection of the blackout curtains, and lived comfortably there.

She wished she could stay with this family until the war was over and done with, but that just wasn't to be. Their home was used as a temporary stop by a Resistance group that concentrated on saving Jews. All too soon, Lovisa showed up on an overcast Sunday morning.

She brought Rika's new documentation, unofficially turning her into "Flora Van der Linden."

"How is Nikolaas?" Rika couldn't keep herself from asking.

"Safe," was all Lovisa would say in a clipped tone. She immediately changed the subject. "Memorize the details on your documentation. For the time being you are to forget you are Rika and become Rosa. You've got a new birth date and everything."

Rika looked at the ID card. Suddenly she was born on March 3, 1927, in Utrecht, not July 28 in Amsterdam. Her father's name was Frederik, her mother's, Anna de Vries.

Lovisa went right on, "A small blue truck will be stopping on the road in front of the house here tomorrow morning at precisely seven o'clock. A newspaper delivery truck. Get in. You'll be taken to your new location." She gave her a little box, the kind that jewelry came in, and said, "And wear this."

With that, Lovisa turned around, left the house, and went on her way on a bicycle.

The box contained a little silver heart necklace engraved with her new name, Rosa, in script. Rika liked it.

"That's why Lovisa is so good at what she does for us," the doctor said. "She concentrates on the big details and also the small ones."

Evy's mother found two additional dresses for Rika/Rosa, ones Evy had outgrown, and let her keep the nightgown that she'd been wearing all week. Rika didn't want to leave, but if she had to, it was good to go with some possessions, few though they were.

"I hope we can get together after the war," Rika told Evy as she folded the dresses into a rucksack. "I've had so much fun here."

"So have I! The last person we helped was about fifty. We'll meet again, Rosa. I promise."

Rika smiled. "Me too."

———○———

IT WENT AS PLANNED.

The following morning Rika got into the back of a van that was loaded with newspapers.

There were two different kinds. The name of an official, Nazi-approved paper was the official cargo of the little truck, and a Resistance paper, along with Rika, were the unofficial ones. The driver didn't say anything at all to her or tell her where they were going. The back of the vehicle had no windows. She didn't have any idea where they were headed.

Rika went over her new "details" to herself. I am Rosa Van der Linden. My father was Frederik, my mother's name was Anna, I was born in Utrecht, and my birth date is March 3, 1927.

The only real fact there was that she really *had* been born in 1927.

At least she was fond of her new name. Evy had picked out such a nice one for her. It could have been a whole lot worse.

It was well over an hour and several delivery stops later when the van finally arrived somewhere or other. The driver opened the back door and Rika, carrying her purse and a rucksack with her dresses and nightgown, got out and blinked in the weak December sunlight.

They were in front of a large and very ornate white house with a mansard roof and plenty of windows. Goodness, Rika thought. A mansion? It was located on what seemed to be a private, out of the way road.

So far so good.

There seemed to be beds of dirt for a garden on either side of the path to the front door, but it was winter. Rika stared at them. Nothing but weeds were growing there at the moment.

"Quickly," the driver said, "follow me. I'm not supposed to be stopping here."

They scurried to the side entrance of the house. The driver, who was carrying a newspaper like a prop, knocked on the door. "Paper delivery," he called out. Then he winked at Rika. "I should say paper delivery plus one."

The door swung open.

It took a full minute before an elderly lady, with blue eyes and her white hair in a bun, opened it. She smiled when she saw them. "Come in," she said.

They did.

"Won't you stay for some tea this time?" She asked the driver. "It's not real tea, of course. It's that unfulfilling herbal kind, but even so."

"You know I can't," the driver said. "I've got to be going."

The lady sighed. "Of course. Thank you stopping by. And for everything." By that, she meant for bringing Rika to her.

———⟨●⟩———

BACK IN AMSTERDAM, Charlotta was lucky to have been set free rather than winding up incarcerated.

She had been questioned for hours on the day the members of the Green Police had taken her to their headquarters for questioning about hiding poor Henk and Kees. Fortunately Bram had already convinced them he hid the boys on his own, without any assistance from anyone else. He had made no mention of Charlotta's involvement, nor had the boys, and they also eliminated the fact that Rika had been secured in another part of the theater.

Charlotta played dumb, though it took a lot of effort. The cops were trying to make her break in half and reveal what she knew. They kept asking her the same questions, over and over, though wording them differently, trying to trip her up.

"I did not know what was going on," she told them repeatedly. "My husband apparently hid people in a room that we keep locked. Why would I check into what was happening in an unused room that had been empty for years? I didn't even have the key for it."

That was a lie on top of a lie, but the cops had no way of knowing it.

Charlotta was ready to burst the whole while she was there being interrogated, wanting to know what had happened to her husband and the Spranger boys, but how could she ask? It was imperative, above all else, to act surprised that Bram had done what he did. How would she ever be able to get out of there and go home to her daughter if they figured out she'd been involved in this "crime" all along? As if doing whatever you could to help your friends' children was a criminal offense in the first place!

It was, though, under the Nazis.

Ridiculous!

Charlotta had another mission while she was stuck at the headquarters. She also wanted to find out, if she could, who had betrayed them in the first place. Was it Corina the floozy next door?

Had it been the horrible Hannus Douw who had seen the kids in the theater? The cops didn't reveal a single clue about the informant.

At one point the two Green Policemen who had been interrogating her left the room, and also left a file about the case on the table.

What to do?

It was so tempting.

She could open the file to see if the name of the informer was in there.

But if the police came back into the room and caught her at it, that could make this into an even bigger disaster than it was already.

Charlotta didn't touch the file.

After eight solid hours of questioning, she was finally released, and told could even reopen the theater, but was informed, in no uncertain terms, they'd be keeping a close watch on her.

"We're not sure if we believe you," the bigger of the two policemen ultimately said. "We just can't prove anything against you. *Yet.*"

It was a threat, but at least she got out of there.

Now it was over a week later.

Charlotta was the new boss of the movie theater and the bookstore and found herself overloaded with work. Old Gerritt had been promoted to her former job of running the refreshment stand, Paolo to taking the tickets. She had found a smart young lady, Ella, to run the Sprangers' bookstore. She even removed her daughter Emmi from her school and sent her to one in another part of town that was run by the nuns, getting her far away from Corina Temmink's two vile daughters. Her friend Betje, the one who ran the box office at the theater, had a daughter there, Lisette, and she was the one who had recommended it.

"My Lisette is thriving there," Betje bragged, "and if you send Emmi to that school, she will at least walk in the door knowing one of the other students."

Charlotta thought that sounded like a rather good idea, sending Emmi to a school where she already had a friend. Any school would have been better than the one the Temminks attended. She had Emmi transferred immediately.

———◦———

BETJE WAS DELIGHTED to hear that Charlotta had put Emmi into Lisette's school.

The ticket seller hadn't been happy, lately, with anything else that was going on regarding Charlotta. Her old friend hadn't been all that accessible to her for a good long time. She'd only approached Betje when she needed something, and even then, all she wanted was a school recommendation for that little know-it-all of hers, Emmi.

Of course, once the police showed up and took Bram away for hiding Jews in the theater, it all made sense. The way Charlotta had seemed to sneak around, always looking sideways or over her shoulder, attempting to become aware of whatever was happening around her and behind her. And that huge bag she had been carrying, claiming it was "lunch" for herself and Bram.

Nonsense! It was a feed bag with supplies for whatever

illegals were living in the theater, more like, Betje thought now. Who could be bothered with anything as distasteful as hiding Jews? She never thought Charlotta would be involved with something like that. Betje was happy that the one good thing the Nazis seemed to be doing was getting *rid* of those people.

She was convinced that Charlotta not only knew what Bram had been doing, but that her old friend almost certainly been involved in it herself, and straight up to her neck.

Betje was mulling over this one night, over a week later, after the theater has been reopened. She was wondering what to do about it. It appalled her that the woman she had thought of as her best friend in the world was involved with helping Jews.

Betje did not like it. Didn't Charlotta known that what she had been doing was wrong?

And just as she was pondering what, if anything, to do about Charlotta, she saw Gerritt's niece Lovisa come along to buy a movie ticket, although she didn't yet know the young woman was related to Gerritt.

"Is Mevrouw Van Der Graaf here tonight?" Lovisa asked Betje, all innocence.

"Yes, she is. She's probably in the back office," Charlotta replied.

She wondered just why Lovisa would need to see her best friend Charlotta.

Jealousy shot through Betje like a white-hot flame.

———◦———

ANOTHER DAY, ANOTHER hiding place.

Rika had to wonder if this would ever end, even though this mansion where she had just been left looked spectacular.

"Won't you come into the dining room, dear?" The gray-haired lady asked Rika. "You're just in time for breakfast."

The furnishings of this house were beautiful, done in the Art Deco style. Lots of curves and rounded lines to everything. Rika glimpsed what she thought were Persian rugs on the floor in the parlor room as she followed her new rescuer down the long hallway. She sat across from her at a table that was set for two.

Their breakfast consisted of thick slices of warm brown bread topped with melted cheese. A delicate teacup was at each of their places and the woman filled it with chamomile tea.

"My name is Greta Coppens. You can call me Tante Greta. We'll say I'm your aunt if anyone asks, yes? Great-aunt, I suppose we should say, given the differences between your age and mine." The woman said it with a gentle smile. "What is your name, dear?"

"Ri – er, I'm Rosa Van der Linden," Rika replied, furious at herself for almost slipping up the very first time she was asked. She took a bite of the bread and cheese and said shyly, "It's really good."

"Thank you, child. I still try, although it's hard these days, with the shortages and the need to go to the black market for anything truly decent. It's bound to become even harder before it's all over, you can be sure of that, too. Before I married my late husband, I was a cook, you know. In this very house, back when the family had servants. There aren't any now."

"Rosa" smiled. "It seems like a really beautiful house."

"And an empty one," Tante Greta said with a touch of sadness. "The Depression hit, and a lot of the family fortune was wiped out. My late husband and I were lucky to be able to keep the house, but we managed. With help from my son, of course. He's in England now, with the members of the Dutch army that managed to sail over there once the occupation started." She brightened and added, "They'll be back, our boys. They'll come back to liberate us. I just wish I knew when."

"So do I," Rika/Rosa agreed.

"Now, then, dear. I suppose you want to discuss what the routine should be for you here," Tante Greta went on. "I wish I didn't have to impose any sort of rules on you at all. You look like a very nice, well-bred girl. But the occupation has changed everything. Oh, well. This is a special occasion, the day of your arrival, so we're eating down here, but usually I think you'll have to stay upstairs. I have a room prepared for you on the third floor. Now, I hate to put you all the way up there. It's an old servant's room. Bathroom is down the hall. If it was up to me you'd be on the second floor, right across from my room, but no, that won't do, not if there's ever a raid. If there is, there's a chifforobe in that room that you can hide in. There's a false back in the chifforobe that leads into the next room, which is a closet, and the door to that is kept locked. Hopefully you won't need to do that. Keep the blackout curtains closed at all times up there, of course."

"I understand," said Rika, though she didn't fully. What in the world was a *chifforobe?*

"Our friends, like the driver who brought you here, you know, *those* friends," she added, meaning the Resistance helpers, without stating it outright, "are going to arrange for schoolbooks for you. I understand you've missed a lot of school already. Too much, really. It's yet another crime of the occupiers, interrupting the schooling of Jewish young people. They've got some of a nerve, if you ask me, coming in here and doing all this. We can try to rectify *that* as soon as possible, at least."

Rika smiled. She liked this Greta Coppens lady already.

After breakfast they went up to Rika's new hideaway. Rika could hardly believe how nice the room was. It had white wallpaper with pink and green stripes. There was a bed, complete with a fluffy pink comforter and even fluffier pillows. A writing desk with a chair. Old Tante Greta had even put some silk flowers in a crystal vase on the bedside table for her. Daffodils. Lovely.

This was a far cry from her old dark lair in the theater.

Tante Greta seemed incredibly gentle and kind. Rika was ready to take the older woman's warmth with open arms.

The chifforobe turned out to be a large closet-like cabinet with drawers on one side and clothes that were hanging from a rod on the other. Several dresses were hanging there already. Her hostess showed her how to push the panel in the back wall of the closet section aside, get into the closet behind it, and slide it back.

"Not many people come here to visit me," Tante Greta went on, sitting down on the chair while Rika sat on the edge of the bed. "The priest comes sometimes. He's my cousin's son. And some of *those* friends. You know the ones. But if you hear that anyone is downstairs, and you will, because I have had an extremely loud doorbell installed on purpose, then into the chifforobe and through to the closet space behind it you go."

"I understand," said Rika.

"Very well, Rosa. I'll leave you to get settled in. You might want to store your things in the closet behind the chifforobe. Better than hanging them inside of it. Those are my old dresses in there and they're rather dated. If anyone asks, I'll simply say I stored them there rather than in my own room."

"Sounds good," Rika agreed. One day, she thought, one day, I'm not going to have to hide my things any longer. And I'm not ever going to have to hide anything about me again, either.

Not if I survive this.

But it was okay for now. What else could it be?

She would be like a tulip bulb in here again, she thought. Trying to thrive under the ground and waiting for the day when she could burst through it and blossom. She would be spending most of her time here in a room with the blackout curtains shut. Although it was comfortable and nice, it wouldn't be getting any sunlight.

"By the way," she asked tentatively, as Tante Greta was almost through the door, "may I ask where I am?"

"Of course, child. This house is located right on the outskirts of Scheveningen."

Scheveningen! It was a famous beach town. Rika had been there several times before the war, back in the good old days, before the world went berserk.

Someday, Rika vowed, when all this is over, I'm going to get there, and I'll see that terrific beach again.

Rika was fifteen years old, just as 1942 was about to turn into 1943, when she settled in at Tante Greta's home and made that promise to herself about one day going to the beach

At seventeen and a half, in the early days of Spring 1945, she still hadn't gotten there yet. But by then, circumstances had begun, at last, to change for the better.

Chapter Nineteen

May 1945
Near Scheveningen and Amsterdam, The Netherlands
and Bay Ridge, Brooklyn, New York

FINALLY THERE WAS HOPE!

It had actually begun almost a year earlier when the Allies had landed on the beaches of Normandy in France on June 6, 1944. That was D-Day. The day when the liberation of Europe from the Nazis had at last begun in earnest!

Paratroopers jumped into occupied France from planes in the early morning hours to get a foothold on the ground. They were followed by British, American, and Canadian troops who sailed in on seven thousand ships and landed onshore.

Seven thousand ships!

Take *that*, Adolf!

The Allies had arrived, at last, to push back the Nazis, and to free the people from their tyrannical reign.

Their progress was slow but steady. They stormed the beaches and began, town by town, to liberate France. It took an agonizingly long time.

Paris wasn't liberated until August.

There were quite a few towns in the southern part of the Netherlands that were liberated that September and October, but then there was a lull. An endless lull, it seemed like. All of the Netherlands still had yet to be freed.

The Allies got bogged down somewhere in Belgium in December, during the Battle of the Bulge. The Germans almost stopped them in their tracks, but try as they might, it didn't work. The Allies kept on fighting. They were the good guys in all this, and Tante Greta said that put them on the side of the angels.

1944 became 1945. Towards the end of April, the Allies still had yet to get to Scheveningen and liberate it, but even so, Rika had a good feeling. They would be arriving soon.

When, oh when, though? Rika kept asking herself, and she wasn't the only Dutch person to wonder. People all over the unliberated parts of the country that were still being bogged down by the Nazis were holding their breaths, with hearts full of hope, waiting for their deliverance.

By then the Nazis were being overpowered in the west as well as the east. The Russians were defeating them in the east, and the rest of the Allies were coming at them from the west. Both sets of armies were inching closer and closer to the German border.

On the 25th of April, both sets of armies met at the Elbe River. In Germany! They hadn't taken Berlin yet, but soon it would all be over.

They had to swing around and liberate the rest of the Netherlands as well. Maybe they were far too preoccupied with Berlin and Germany.

In the meantime, the situation was far from ideal for the Dutch. In fact, it was even worse than usual. That was due to an idea the Dutch government in exile had come up with, in Britain, when they had encouraged the railway workers to go on strike in order to try and interfere with German troop movements by train.

It backfired, and the Nazis, of course, wanted to get the Dutch back for it. Therefore, in one of the most vicious revenge plots ever enacted in all of recorded history, the Germans stopped delivering foodstuffs to the western part of the Netherlands. It was a deliberate blockade.

It hadn't helped that that the winter of 1944-1945 was unusually cold. The waterways were frozen solid, on top of everything else. The bastard Nazis had stopped supplies from coming in on the trains, which was bad enough, but due to the deep freezes, food also could not get delivered to the people over the water.

People were calling it "The Hunger Winter."

The people of Amsterdam were dying from starvation in droves, it was said. That made Rika concerned for her old protector Charlotta Van Der Graaf and her daughter, Emmi.

It was happening affecting Tante Greta and Rika's area of the country, too.

Only recently had the sadistic Nazis finally allowed the Canadian air force to start dropping food parcels to the Dutch people. Tante Greta had said, when they heard about it on the BBC, "They must know they're losing now, and are afraid they'll be held to account for it."

That sounded right to Rika. The Germans hadn't previously cared one whit.

Fortunately the food situation wasn't too bad at Tante Greta's place. It wasn't that great, either, but they weren't starving to death. This was due to Greta's foresight. She had stockpiled supplies, little by little, and had always enjoyed preserving fruits and vegetables. She had started this, with Rika's help, long before the blockade began.

"When the end of the war comes," she had told Rika many times, "there will probably be a national descent into chaos, at least until everything straightens out. We have to be prepared for even worse shortages than we've got on our hands now."

Prepared they were!

Several times, friends from the Resistance had stopped by with gifts of food supplies they had grown in their own gardens to help supplement Greta and Rika's coffers. Rika had only met one of them, the priest, Father Josephus, Greta's relative, and the only person they felt they could trust completely. Rika had gone straight to her room, and retreated through the secret panel in the chifforobe to the closet behind it, whenever anyone else showed up. These precautions may have been extreme, but they remained necessary, especially since they were so close to being freed.

On May 1st they heard an amazing bit of news and found out they were even closer to deliverance than they thought.

Rika was in the kitchen helping Greta make some apple jam when Father Josephus stopped by the house.

"Haven't you ladies been listening to the radio?" He asked them.

When they responded with blank looks, he exulted, "Adolf Hitler is *kaput!*"

"What?" Asked Tante Greta, with her eyes widening with a touch of joy at the prospect.

"How?" Rika wanted to know.

"The coward's way out, that's how," laughed the priest. "He died by his own hand. Suicide. Shot himself. Berlin is completely surrounded by the Russians, according to the BBC, and that monster didn't want to fall into their hands. Oh, no! Otherwise he would have had to face the consequences of what he's done. *All* of them."

Rika grinned. "He probably would have even had to go before a Russian military tribunal, if he'd lived."

"Exactly," agreed Father Josephus. "Where he is now, you can be sure, it's boiling hot, and he can't keep the war going from the depths of Hell. It won't be long now!"

And it wasn't.

"Yes, surely the end is near if that madman is out of the way," added Tante Greta. "It was a pity the assassination attempt on him last summer by his own generals never worked or we'd have been out of this sooner."

One of the generals had tried to blow Hitler up at a meeting with a bomb hidden in a briefcase.

On May 4th the announcement the entire country had been waiting for finally, *finally* came.

It was broadcast on the radio early that evening, and it was a moment that Rika was never, ever to forget.

The Germans had unconditionally surrendered the German armed forces in the Netherlands to British Field Marshal Sir Bernard Montgomery!

And it was not just the end of hostilities in the Netherlands. Northwest Germany and Denmark were included in this surrender, too!

The ceasefire was going to take place the very next day, May 5th, at 12:00 Noon.

Unconditional surrender!

In Dutch, it was quite a mouthful, *onvoorwaardelijke overgave*.

But it was the most beautiful phrase Rika had ever heard.

———⊙———

UP IN AMSTERDAM, AT the same time, Charlotta and her daughter Emmi heard the broadcast, too. They almost fainted with relief, not to mention hunger.

Surrender at last!

The last few days the mother and daughter had been doing a bit better. The merciful Canadians had airdropped thousands of pounds of food to the people of Amsterdam. Charlotta was skin and bones and so was Emmi, by that point, since the Hunger Winter had hit both of them hard, but now there was actually *something to eat*. Emmi had caught one of the food packages that had been dropped.

The contents of the package seemed nothing short of miraculous. Flour, margarine, coffee! Milk powder, cheese, *chocolate!* Charlotta had almost forgotten such treasures still existed, yet now, from out of the sky, here they were!

"Slowly," Charlotta advised Emmi, "we must eat these good things slowly. We've been deprived of decent food for so long that I don't want either one of us getting a stomachache from this."

"I can't help myself," her weakened daughter, now thirteen, replied. She all but tore into a bar of chocolate and finished the whole thing in less than a minute.

Within the hour, poor Emmi was doubled over with pains from eating all of it, but at least she had finally received some nourishment.

"You'll just have to tough it out," Charlotta advised. She wished she had some medicine to give her daughter to ease the pain but there wasn't any.

"This is no way to celebrate the ceasefire," Emmi griped, lying on her stomach in her bed.

"Get through tonight and we can rejoice tomorrow," replied her ever practical mother, giving Emmi a glass of water. For once Charlotta had a slight smile on her face.

It wasn't that she was happy her child was in pain. She wasn't. That was tearing her to shreds inside.

The hint of a smile came with the thought of the *onvoorwaardelijke overgave*.

The end of hostilities was what came first, she knew. After that, maybe she would be able to find out some answers about whatever had happened to the others. Her husband, Bram. The Spranger boys, Henk and Kees. Their father, Julius. And where was Rika? She wasn't sure of that, and Lovisa, her Resistance contact, had disappeared in the last few weeks. She wanted to find out where Lovisa was, too.

Gerritt also was concerned about Lovisa. He hadn't revealed it before, when the war was raging, but once it was over, he approached Charlotta and confided to her that the woman he had referred her to go and see, back when she needed hiding places for Nikolaas and Rika, was his niece.

Hopefully the young member of the Resistance had not been arrested, or worse, executed, right as the end had almost arrived.

And now the end of the war was *here*.

They had a package of food.

There was an unconditional surrender.

Charlotta could hardly believe it. Everything had finally turned around!

——————⊙——————

FAR AWAY, AND ACROSS the mighty Atlantic Ocean, Florentine Spranger heard the astonishingly good news about the surrender at her flower shop on Third Avenue in the Bay Ridge section of Brooklyn, New York, too. It came over the radio.

Florentine had been putting together an arrangement of white carnations and violets for a wedding, and she burst into loud, astonished tears.

Celeste Mancini, her assistant, came running out of the back room, where she had been sorting a shipment of roses by color. "Florentine! What is it? Has something happened?"

It took Florentine a full minute to recover enough to say, "Yes! Something good! The Nazis are surrendering in the Netherlands!"

Celeste clapped her hands and beamed. "At last! At last! Your husband and your other children will be free to come here and join you!"

The two friends embraced.

Florentine could only hope that this would prove to be true.

——————⊙——————

FATHER JOSEPHUS STILL had more good news to impart to Tante Greta and Rika.

"The Canadians are coming into Scheveningen today to take over from the Germans," he exulted. "Want to go into town with me? Everybody of goodwill everywhere is hoping to be there and greet them!"

"Except for the collaborators, of course," Rika smiled.

Could this be true?

Was she really about to get the chance to go outside, to visit Scheveningen, and see the lovely beach town she had dreamed of visiting again for so long?

"Of course we'll go with you," Greta beamed. "After so many years of war, we're not going to miss *this!*"

Rika, who still wasn't sure just where the house was located in terms of its proximity to Scheveningen, asked how they were going to get there.

"Don't you know? We're right on the outskirts of it. It's a bit out of the way, maybe three kilometers, but it's still within walking distance, Rosa," the priest explained to her.

"Rika," she corrected him in a small little voice.

Had she finally said it? Her real name?

Oh, what a pleasure it was to say her actual, real, *true* name! The one she'd been given from her mother and father!

"Excuse me?" Father Josephus asked, not comprehending.

In a stronger and more assured voice, the girl explained, "I could never tell either one of you. My name isn't Rosa Van der Linden at all, as nice as that one is. I'm really Rika Spranger."

"It's a pleasure to finally formally meet you, then, Rika Spranger," Tante Greta said right away, with a grin. "That's a pretty name, too."

"It certainly is," Father Josephus agreed with a smile. "I like it."

"And I knew all along you were using a fake name," Greta added, "out of necessity, not desire, so don't you ever feel guilty about it. Rika."

Rika had felt terrible about it, lying about who she was to this good lady all this time, so what Tante Greta said came as a relief.

"You weren't the only one to do that," said the priest, "I can tell you that much."

Rika and Greta put on their coats, gathered their purses, and went outside.

It was, incredibly, the first time Rika had been out of the house since the day she had arrived.

The first things she spotted were three tulips, two whites and a pink. They had sprouted up by the door.

Rika all but bounded into the front yard, basking in the golden sunshine gilding the new green leaves on the trees and looking up at the lovely light blue Northern sky. It was such a beautiful spring day, and in so many more ways than one!

The girl who had been kept indoors for so long couldn't help herself. She called out in an even louder, happier voice, to the trees and the sun and the sky, "Hello again, world! Here I am! I'm Rika, I'm Rika, *I'm Rika!*"

With that, she held out her arms and spun around and around in a circle, filled with the sparkling joy of long-awaited release.

Chapter Twenty

May 1945
Near Scheveningen and Amsterdam, The Netherlands
and Bay Ridge, Brooklyn, New York

It turned out to be one of the most amazing afternoons of their lives. White fluffy blossoms were blooming on many of the trees the trio passed on their way to the center of Scheveningen.

The town had taken a beating, in some sections, from German bombs, like plenty of others places all over the continent, but Scheveningen was still there, beach, rubble, damaged buildings and all. On many nights in hiding Rika had heard the German planes flying overhead, dropping bombs somewhere in the distance. They'd frightened her half to death, but she was still here, too. Dutch tricolor flags of red, white and blue, not the vile Nazi occupiers' black, white and red ugly swastika banner, had appeared and were flying from so many Scheveningen windows and flag poles, a welcome, much loved and remembered sight. They had been banned by the Nazis but now they were back. Ha, so was I, Rika thought with a smile.

She even saw some girls wearing orange ribbons in their hair. Orange! She wished she had one of those ribbons for herself and said so.

And the ocean! Her first sight of it, in the distance, brought tears to her eyes.

I've finally made it, she thought happily, there it is! There's the sea!

What an incredible feeling! She was where she had dreamed of being for so, so long.

Crowds of people were lining the sidewalk of a wide main street, waiting in joyful anticipation for the first sight of their liberators.

A man and woman, standing on either side of a pale teenage boy about her age, came to stand next to Rika, Greta and Father Josephus. "It's all right, Avram," the woman was saying to the boy. "No more hiding for you!"

Rika looked at the boy with more interest after she heard that. When was the last time she'd even been around a young boy?

Tante Greta heard it, as well. "He was in hiding? So was this one," she smiled, indicating Rika. "We should get them together."

"Feels strange, doesn't it?" The boy said in a whisper.

"It does," Rika nodded, "but this is a day to rejoice!"

"You don't have to whisper any longer, either, Avram," the woman said to him.

"Give him time," said the man, "he just got out of our cellar."

"Rika here is out for the first time too," laughed Father Josephus, "but you should have seen her. She was shouting her real name to the trees and sky. You should try it, Avram!"

Avram could only smile shyly, then averted his eyes. He looked afraid of his own shadow. He didn't say a word.

Suddenly the could all hear a rumbling coming from one end of the street.

The crowd seemed to hold its collective breath for a moment.

Then, as the first tank finally appeared along the street like a dream come true, they all started to cheer as one.

Even Avram.

———— ◉ ————

AT HOME THAT NIGHT on 84th Street in Brooklyn, Florentine's two youngest children could barely contain their excitement.

"When will they be here?" Reenie asked, cutting right to the heart of the matter. "When can we see Rika, Henk, Kees and Daddy again?"

The girl had been totally Americanized. She'd never called her father "Daddy" in Holland, but that was what the Brooklyn kids called theirs, so she always referred to Julius as "Daddy" now.

"We should get bunk beds to put in my room," Billy added, "for Henk and Kees. I'll share a room with them again!" He had really missed their company.

"And get a twin bed for my room, for Rika," Reenie bubbled. "Oh, I can't wait until I see her again!" She and her older sister had once been close, although it was now rather hard for Reenie to remember what that had been like.

Florentine tried to tamp down their enthusiasm. "Slow down! We have to wait and see," she told them. She knew caution was called for. She was hopeful, but couldn't get too far ahead of the situation. Florentine didn't want to spell it out too much for Billy and Reenie, who were now thirteen and fourteen years old, but she had heard some rather horrific rumors over the past few years about the persecution of Jews, and others, in Europe. The Nazis were brutal. Always deporting people to Nazi occupied Poland.

And why *Poland?*

Were her children there?

It was impossible to know what had gone on yet, or if the rest of the family was safe. There had been no word.

With any luck, she would be hearing from them soon.

———— ◉ ————

LATER THAT NIGHT IN Amsterdam, sounds of revelry were drifting in from the street. A group of people went by singing a joyful rendition of "Oranje Boven."

Emmi had finally fallen into a fitful sleep, still in misery after consuming the chocolate bar, while Charlotta lay awake.

Her heart was still rejoicing over the unconditional surrender.

Yet her head was flying, or so it seemed, in a whole other direction.

Who had betrayed Bram, Henk and Kees?

That was the question.

She was determined to find out the answer.

There was the slut who lived next door, Corina Temmink.

Her two children.

The man who'd fallen asleep in the theater that time, Douw.

They were the ones she knew about.

But might there have been someone else?

There were others who worked in the theater. She trusted Gerritt completely.

But what about Paolo, the young boy who had worked there? He no longer did. He had been taken in a roundup to work in Germany two years earlier, not long after Rika and Nikolaas left.

Betje she trusted as well, since they'd been friends for so long.

Then there were the projectionists, Gustav and Bartel. Had they seen anything? Heard anything? The projection booth was right across the hallway from Rika's hiding place. But it wasn't Rika whose hiding place had been reported.

And there had been customers, all the time, in and out of the theater. They were supposed to stay in the public areas, the auditorium, lobby, and the rest rooms. They were not permitted to go gallivanting all over the building, yet sometimes, it was inevitable, people strayed from wherever they were allowed to go. It was possible one of them had gotten loose and heard something suspicious near where the boys were, backstage.

It had been especially true later in the war when there'd been several bombing raids, with patrons leaving the building in the. Middle of a movie to get to the air raid shelter down the block, and returning when the all-clear sounded to watch it to the end, but by then, Bram and the boys had already been discovered.

Even so.

It was beginning to look to Charlotta like there weren't just a few possible informers to choose from.

There may have been, literally, dozens.

Charlotta tossed, turned, and sighed. The important thing, first of all, wasn't the identity of the betrayer. It was to answer the other pressing question, which was where were Bram, Kees, and Henk? She wanted them to come home. She also had to wonder about Julius Spranger.

She heard from Lovisa, before the girl vanished, that both Nikolaas and Rika were still alive and thriving somewhere, the last Lovisa had heard.

After everyone she cared about was accounted for, though, Charlotta still wanted to find out who the betrayer was, and if there was any possibility to obtain some justice for what that accursed individual did, she was going to get it.

Chapter Twenty-One

May 1945
Near Scheveningen and Amsterdam, The Netherlands
and Bay Ridge, Brooklyn, New York

————————◉————————

IT WAS ALL OVER, FINALLY, totally, completely, one hundred percent over, by May 8th.

The day was hailed as V-E Day, "Victory in Europe." The surrender had been signed, and half the world, literally, was ready to celebrate.

The good news of the unconditional surrender unleashed the biggest collection of simultaneous parties the world had ever seen.

Never mind that there had been so many deaths, both civilian and military, or that thousands of people had been bombed out of their homes, or deported, or were among the missing. It would all have to be faced.

But not on VE Day. That was to be a day reserved for festivities.

In Amsterdam there were parades and parties and dancing in the street. Charlotta and Emmi, who had finally recovered from eating the chocolate bar, were outside cheering along with everyone else.

At one point they saw Dutch women who had slept with Nazis getting their hair shaved off, until they looked bald, and were marched through the streets as "*moffenmeiden*," German sluts. "Moffen" was a slur used for the Germans, similar to what they heard some Canadian soldiers calling them, "Krauts." There were men who collaborated that were taken away by the police. People were not inclined to be forgiving where the collaborators and traitors were concerned. All of this transpired right on the streets, alongside of the parties, parades, and celebrations.

Charlotta wasn't at all shocked to see that the woman who lived next to their theater, Corina Temmink, was one of the *moffenmeiden*. Well, that figures, Charlotta thought. She slept with lots of men. But why with the enemy, too?

Charlotta had to wonder where Corina's daughters were while their mother was on the receiving end of retribution out on the street. Were Neeltje and Lena home alone, fending for themselves? Or where?

"Charlotta! Emi!" A familiar voice rang out, interrupting her thoughts about Corina's children.

It was Betje and her daughter, Lisette. They joined Charlotta and Emmi and watched the parade with them.

"Maybe now," Betje smiled, "our lives can return to normal." *Our friendship, too,* she thought, but didn't say.

"Ha, what's normal any longer?" Charlotta asked, halfway laughing it off. The country had been decimated. The Nazis had stolen so much from the Dutch, not to mention from every country they had invaded in Europe. Normalcy had become an alien concept.

Charlotta didn't notice the disappointed look in Betje's eyes as she said it. She wasn't looking for it. A contingent bearing the good old Dutch flag were marching down the street singing, and she got distracted by the wonderful sight of that.

Later on that evening there were dances in the streets. A man with an accordion was playing music in front of their apartment building. Henrietta Blazer offered Emmi and Charlotta champagne, but after Emmi's too much, too soon ordeal with the chocolate, they gave it a pass. Their systems were too used to near-starvation rations to drink something alcoholic, though they wished they could on such a special night.

Emmi danced with her mother, amazed that the war had ended, and thinking maybe, just maybe, soon her father Bram would come home from wherever he'd been sent, and Nikolaas, too, and then, maybe, all would be well.

Maybe.

———— ◉ ————

REENIE AND BILLY BEGGED Florentine to let them go to Manhattan and see what was going on in Times Square. Celeste Mancini's two children, Susan and Tommy, announced they were up for the same thing.

Even Florentine and Celeste liked the idea. They closed the flower shop for the day and went along with their children on the subway.

Times Square had never seemed so crowded with people before, thousands and thousands of them, and every last one was in a celebratory mood. Florentine was too, of course. After so many years of war and the continuing uncertainties about her family, how could she not be?

Of all the shenanigans that were going on, the one Florentine liked the best was a man who was waving around a roll of toilet paper. "Here's to the end!" He kept saying. "Here's to the end!" The kids thought he was hilarious.

But then she saw a Western Union office and knew exactly what she wanted to do, first, to enjoy this remarkable day. "I'll be right back," she told the others, and dashed inside.

She sent one telegram after another. One to Julius, one to Kees, one to Henk, and one to Rika, all to her old address in Amsterdam where, presumably, they still lived.

She sent another one to Bram and Charlotta Van Der Graaf.

All of the ones to her family contained the same message in Dutch:

———— ◉ ————

HELLO MY DARLINGS FROM Brooklyn
Waiting to hear from Julius Kees Henk Rika

Please reply immediately
Lots of Love Florentine Spranger

————— ◉ —————

THE ONE TO THE VAN Der Graafs was only slightly edited:

————— ◉ —————

WAITING TO HEAR FROM you and my family
   Please reply immediately
   Love to you all
   Florentine Spranger

————— ◉ —————

THERE! THE TELEGRAMS even contained the address where they could reply. She gave the one for the shop.

After she sent her messages, she felt a whole lot better, and a lot freer inside to enjoy the day.

With so many people in the square she was lucky to find her little group again. They only stayed there for about an hour because the euphoria was borderline crazy. Besides, there were a lot of people toasting with alcohol and getting plastered. It wasn't the best place for the kids.

So Florentine treated everyone to burgers at a restaurant, and later they even went to see a movie, *Brewster's Millions*.

Tomorrow will be better, Florentine thought.

Not simply due to the war in Europe being over, though the conflict with Japan was still ongoing and that mess had yet to be settled.

By tomorrow I might even have a response to my telegrams!

————— ◉ —————

TANTE GRETA SAID THAT, since she'd twisted her ankle during the walk home, on the day they went to the center of Scheveningen to see the Canadians roll in, she wasn't up for attending the VE Day celebrations.

Rika had wanted to go, but strangely, not without Tante Greta.

"Oh Rosa, I mean, Rika," the woman said to her, "you shouldn't *not* go to the celebrations because of me. You've had to wait long enough to get out there, have fun, and live like a normal girl."

Rika was tempted, but she still wasn't positive if it was such a good idea. The day they'd gone to see the Canadians, she had followed the other two to the center of town. She hadn't bothered memorizing the twisting route they took to get there and back. The girl had no idea of the layout of the area, and she hesitated.

It was a good thing that she did, because all of a sudden, there was a knock on Tante's front door.

Quite a knock. It came as a happy little rhythm, almost like a song. Dum-dum dee-dum-dum, dum *dum!*

"Who in the world is that?" Tante Greta asked as she made her way to answer it.

Force of habit caused Rika to hang back, in the parlor and out of sight of the doorway. She realized it would probably be a long time before she got used to *not* having to fear a knock on the door.

"Hello there," she heard Tante Greta greeting whoever was outside on the doorstep. She was using a tone of surprise at the sight. "May I help you?"

That was curious. Who was she finding it unusual to see?

"I hope so," chirped a voice that, all of a sudden, Rika remembered. "I'm Evy Achtenberg, and I'm looking for my old pal Rosa Van Der Linden!"

Rika could hardly believe it.

"Evy!" Her friend's wonderful name came flying out of Rika's mouth before she could stop it. She couldn't help her feet from rushing to the door, either, and all but skipped there with a great big smile on

her face. Evy, the one friend she'd made during her whole ordeal! "How did you know I was here?"

"How do you think, silly?" Evy replied, with her good old grin and a shake of her head. The braids were gone. Now she had a stylish shoulder-length haircut and looked all grown up, save for the look in her eyes. She was still good old mischievous Evy. "My parents and I were part of the Resistance group that placed you here, that's how," Evy laughed as the two girls embraced. "And remember? We promised we'd get together again after the war."

"I couldn't believe my eyes," Tante Greta said at that point, "seeing there was a young girl coming to visit. So *you're* Evy
Achtenberg! The doctor's daughter. Your family is famous to our whole group."

Evy made a little curtsy as if she was taking a bow on a stage. "That's me! Evy Achtenberg, the one and only!"

Tante Greta laughed.

"I never knew your last name before," Rika said to Evy.

"I couldn't tell you for security reasons," Evy said.

"Oh, and you don't know my name, either. It's Rika Spranger."

"Evy and Rika," Tante Greta suggested, "why don't I make us some tea, and serve you what passes for rationed bread these days, along with my homemade jam? And then the two of you can go and enjoy the parade, or whatever they're doing in town to celebrate VE Day." Then she thought of something else. "Oh, and you might want to stop by a red brick house with blue shutters that's at the far end of this road first."

"Certainly, if you want us to, but why?" Rika asked.

"Why? That's where the boy we met the other day has been hiding. That shy boy, Avram. The nice couple who were sheltering him told me where they live, hoping maybe you might visit him, Rika. He's very skittish because, if you can believe this, he was hidden in no less than *ten* different locations, but if you and Evy show up, maybe you could persuade him to go along with you."

"That's awful about the ten hiding places, so he's coming with us," Evy smiled. "I'm going to make sure of it."

"So will I," agreed Rika.

It was while they were on the way to Avram's hideout house that Evy told Rika about the mystery in Amsterdam regarding Lovisa, the Resistance contact who helped to hide Jews.

"Nobody knows what happened to her," Evy said. "Two weeks ago she just disappeared." Evy shook her head. "Right when it was almost at the end of the war, too."

Rika found this news disturbing. She remembered Lovisa, the young woman who had arranged for her and Nikolaas to get onto the barge when they had to get out of Amsterdam. "Does anyone have any idea about what happened?"

"Oh, yes, there's plenty of guesses, and theories, but there's not a single bit of proof about any of them. Nobody saw her get picked up by the authorities or anything. She was based at a restaurant, where it was easy for people to contact her if they needed a place to hide or anything else our group could help them with. She left one evening to go home from there and she never arrived. Hasn't been seen since." Evy gave Rika a pointed look. "When you get back to Amsterdam, maybe could you see if you can find anything out?"

"*Naturlich,*" Rika replied. Of course she would. It was the least she could do after all the good Lovisa had brought into her life.

Yet the thought of returning to Amsterdam gave her a pang. She liked it here, living with Tanta Greta.

She didn't really like the idea of going away and leaving the sweet older lady all alone. With a mother and two siblings in America, and a father and two other siblings who had been carted away to who-knew-where by the Nazis, what kind of a home could there be in Amsterdam for her now anyway?

She had to wonder. Would the lost members of of her family ever be found?

Chapter Twenty-Two

May 1945
Near Scheveningen and Amsterdam, The Netherlands
and Bay Ridge, Brooklyn, New York

Charlotta was astounded to receive Florentine Spranger's telegram. Happy, too. Florentine! It felt like old times to hear from her.

It didn't arrive until three full days after it had been sent in New York City, probably due to the local celebrations of the victory on the one hand and the major disruptions in services in Amsterdam on the other. Many roads were impassible all over the country, especially after the battles that had ensued at the end as the Canadians drove out the *Duitsers*. The accursed Germans hadn't just retreated and gone home, oh, no. They'd blown up bridges and flooded dykes first. It was outrageous. A lot of times the electricity was cut off in one place or another, as well. Phone lines were down in some places. Probably telegraph lines too.

So many malfunctioning services! Anything could have caused the delay in the delivery.

But it finally came.

A telegram from Florentine! It was like receiving a message in a bottle in reverse from an exile on a desert island, Charlotta thought. Florentine was alive and well and living in Brooklyn. No occupation, no *Duitsers*, and none of the atrocities they'd brought along with them, either. *Charlotta* had been the one who had felt like she was lost to civilization the whole time the Nazis had been in Holland.

At least they were gone now.

But how was she to answer the telegram? Charlotta, as yet, had no idea where any of them were. There had been no word from Rika. Had she been captured too? Charlotta normally could have gone straight to Lovisa to inquire about where the girl had been hidden, except now *Lovisa* was among the missing. What a thing to have happen!

What a continuing mess.

As for Julius and the boys, not to mention her husband Bram, too, all four of them might have been sent to Germany to work, or to those dreaded camps in Poland where, the terrible news was emerging, so many innocent people had been murdered. They hadn't just naturally died.

At the moment, Charlotta just didn't know anything about any of them.

She had to answer the telegram, however. Poor Florentine must have been going out of her mind awaiting news of her husband and children. There was a store where she could send a wire back to her on the way to opening up the theater for the day.

Charlotta just hated the whole idea of having to reply with the truth, which was, "No news yet."

———◉———

"MY DEAR," TANTE GRETA said to Rika that same afternoon as they sat beside one another at the table, sipping tea. "I so enjoy having you here. Please don't take what I'm about to say the wrong way. But don't you think it's time you went home?"

"Home?" Rika repeated.

"Yes, child. Home. You're a city girl from Amsterdam, aren't you?"

Rika had not told Tante Greta too much about her situation, believing the less anyone knew about it, the better. The woman knew the girl came from Amsterdam, and that she had a mother, sister and brother in America, but that was about it. Rika had never mentioned how her father had been taken away, or how her brothers were discovered while in hiding, or any of it.

"Yes, but, it's rather complicated," she began.

"You know you can tell me anything," Tante Greta said to her gently, taking her hand.

So Rika began to relay the whole tale to her. Her father's arrest when he tried to buy them false documentation. The Van Der Graafs, who had hidden her in their theater. The betrayal. How Bram had been arrested at the theater along with her brothers. The way Charlotta had gotten her out of there right beforehand, just in the nick of time. All of it. The whole hideous story.

Just telling it to Greta brought up memories Rika wished she could forget. Her wonderful Papa, so hopeful of getting them new identities and resettling in another town, out from under the Nazi threat. Charlotta, that first morning in hiding, bringing her apple fritters. Bram, explaining how she should hide under a blanket, face away from the door, and read books using a flashlight. Her brothers who had managed, through Charlotta, to get her a birthday cake on the day she turned fifteen.

And her mother, Florentine, on the long-ago day in 1939, before she left for America, buying Rika the little hat that she had cherished, mainly because it was the last time Mama had given her a gift. She wondered what had happened to it.

Tante Greta had tears in her eyes by the time Rika finished. "What you are describing. It's worse than I ever imagined, child. I won't try to say that it isn't. It is."

Rika said she appreciated Tante Greta's honesty.

"We need to see Father Josephus," Tante Greta decided. "He'll know how you can proceed. We must try to contact your mother, at least, and this Charlotta woman, too. We can go to see him in about an hour, today, if that would work for you."

"It would," said Rika. She had no other plans, especially now that Evy had returned home, although sitting outside and just looking at the trees and the spring flowers on Greta's property gave her more pleasure than she could ever express to anyone who hadn't been hidden.

"As a matter of fact," Tante Greta continued, "we should even go to Sunday Mass at Father's church this weekend. I'm not trying to convert you or anything, mind. I wouldn't do that to you. I simply think it might be good for you to be out among other people and get to meet some of those who live nearby. You also might like to see Father Josephus in action when he's on the pulpit. He's a very good speaker."

"I can believe it," Rika said with a small smile, though she felt rather sad after having spoken about her situation.

Tante Greta noticed. "I can't promise you there will be a happy ending, my good girl. After a war, they often don't exist. I still remember the aftereffects of the first one. But I will certainly do my best to help you find out what your next steps should be, and you can stay with me as long as you like, until we can get you to America, to your mother."

America! Rika smiled at the very idea.

She thought of how her father had started having her light the Sabbath candles on Friday nights after the persecutions began. "Would it be possible," she asked, "if I could light the candles this Friday night in thanks to God for bringing me through? It's a tradition in my religion."

"Of course, child!"

So that was the beginning of Rika lighting the Sabbath candles again on Fridays.

———— ◉ ————

FATHER JOSEPHUS USHERED Greta and her lovely charge into his office and shut the door.

Not that anyone else was in the rectory. No one was, but sometimes there were walk-ins who needed pastoral advice, and from the solemn looks on the faces of Greta and Rika, he knew it wouldn't do to get interrupted.

He was as astonished as Greta had been to hear the girl's full story. Missing father, two missing brothers, and a missing protector, too!

Plus a mother in America, yet. And two more siblings.

That part about the mother was the good news, he thought. The mother was probably alive, well and safe, not to mention worried half sick about her daughter. Surely she would want this girl to come to the United States as soon as it was possible. He just wondered how soon they could make that happen.

As for her father, the brothers and the protector who had all been taken away, Father Josephus did not want to say it, but by now the world knew about the concentration camps, and he was afraid that was where all four of them may have ended up.

Some of them really had been labor camps like the Germans had claimed they were.

But others were extermination centers. Evil, hideous places where people from groups the Germans didn't like, and were too old or too young to be put to work, or farmed out to help the war effort, got sent straight to be killed. In gas chambers.

So that was why those "summonses" had been issued to teens, children, old people and orphans. They weren't really being sent to do any kind of war effort work, just as so many people had suspected.

They were sent to their deaths.

Still others, the able-bodied, really were selected to work in some of those places.

Worked to death, in many cases.

It was the sickest revelation to come out of this war yet.

Survivors of those camps were beginning to trickle back into Holland, now that the hostilities had ended, and most arrived bone thin, weakened, and in terrible shape. A woman from Scheveningen had returned and was taken straight to the hospital by the ticket seller at the station who saw her shuffling off the train. It wasn't known yet if the doctors would be able to save her life, and to think that that lady was one survivor story among far too many among the few that had begun trickling home.

Father Josephus hoped, and would pray, Rika's father, brothers, and the man who had sheltered her, had all somehow been spared this fate. He just had a feeling it wasn't too likely.

"I've heard that the Dutch Red Cross is going to be collecting information about the people who were displaced during the war and will start trying to reunite them with their families. We'll have to get you registered with them. They're going to have a massive job on their hands, so it might take some time before you hear anything. For now," he said to the girl, using an upbeat tone, "let's go send some telegrams, shall we? My treat. You can use as many words in them as you like."

And, as Greta's ankle still wasn't quite right from their last sojourn into Scheveningen, he rigged up a small cart to the old donkey he kept in the rectory stables, and they rode to town in that.

———◉———

IT WAS THE SATURDAY afternoon following VE Day. A warm, pleasant, partly cloudy day in Brooklyn, New York.

Florentine was at the flower shop, and Billy and Reenie were there to help her.

There were so many orders for floral arrangements these days! Soldiers stationed overseas were sending one wire after another, ordering bouquets to be sent to their mothers, or sweethearts, or wives, now that communications between Europe and America were back open again.

Billy was constantly going in and out, making deliveries on his bicycle, with the wrapped flowers placed in the basket. The shop was more prosperous than ever.

If only another telegram would come from Holland, Florentine had thought. One with good news. A day earlier she had received the message that had come from her old friend Charlotta Van Der Graaf, and it had left her terribly discouraged.

———— ◉ ————

FLORENTINE GREAT HEARING from you
Still awaiting news of Henk Kees
both our husbands Rika and my son Nikolaas
will wire as soon as I hear anything
Love to you Verena and Willem
Charlotta Van Der Graaf and Emmi

———— ◉ ————

FLORENTINE WAS SO HAPPY to know Charlotta and Emmi, at least, were alive, but what had happened to the others? Had they been deported? All of them?

If so, this may have been the end of a war, but it would also be the start of a personal nightmare. One that was unimaginable.

Florentine tried to remain positive, for the sake of Reenie and Billy, at least, but it wasn't exactly easy for her. She had quietly cried herself to sleep the night before.

"Here's another one," the same messenger who had brought two more telegrams to the shop already that morning said as he came through the door, making the little bells that hung from the inside jangle, and handed it to Reenie. "For your mother."

That particular messenger, eighteen-year-old Monty, loved being sent to the flower shop. Blonde Reenie Spranger was adorable. If only she was a little bit older than fifteen, he would have asked her out for a date and taken her to get an ice cream soda.

"I'm back here," Florentine said, emerging from the back room, after she had just taken some violets out of the refrigerator where the fresh flowers were stored. She gave the messenger a nickel tip.

Monty was about to leave the shop, but liked to remain in Reenie's presence, so he lingered by a display of lilacs in vases, wondering if maybe he should splurge on some flowers for his mother.

Reenie had already torn the telegram open. "Look, Mom! This one, it's from Holland, from Scheveningen!"

"What's that?" Florentine asked, putting the violets on the counter, both her ears and her spirits perking up at the sound of the name of the Dutch beach town.

"You won't believe this!" Reenie added as she read it. A huge smile was lighting up her face and she seemed overjoyed. "Billy, Mom, come here! Wow!"

"Let me see that," Florentine urged, all but knocking her daughter over by accident as she rushed to take a look at the communication that had arrived from across the sea.

———————◉———————

GREETINGS MAMA VERENA and Willem
    Survived in hiding near Scheveningen
    with Greta Coppens also was hid with brothers
    by Van Der Graafs in theater
    Felt like a tulip bulb living underground
    but all turned out well
    Not sure yet where others are
    Wire me back I love you all
    Oranje boven
    Your daughter and sister
    Rika Spranger

———————◉———————

SUDDENLY MONTY WASN'T sure what had happened.

All he knew was that the three Sprangers were crying, then laughing, then hugging, all three. He knew it was good news.

The very best kind, for a change.

So many times during the war Monty had delivered devastating messages to families. This soldier was missing. That one was dead. It went on and on and it never became any easier for him to hear their sobs and wails.

This was different. Reenie finally turned to him and explained, "Our sister is alive!"

"We're going to bring her here," Billy added.

"She was in hiding all this time!" Florentine smiled, sounding enormously relieved, as delighted tears ran down her face. "And that signature line! *Oranje boven!*" She took it as an indication that, in spite of everything, Rika's spirit hadn't been broken.

The two children began to sing the "Oranje Boven" song in the Dutch that they had barely remembered until that very moment.

Monty found himself reluctant to leave the happy scene.

"Let's bring out the soda pop and have a toast," Reenie suggested. "You too, Monty, stay and join us!"

"Monty, you are the bearer of the best news I've received since the war began!" Florentine exclaimed. "Thank you!"

"I'd love to stay," Monty grinned. And yes, he decided, he would also buy those lilacs for his mother.

Maybe he could even take Reenie to the ice cream parlor after all, too. He really wasn't *that much* older than she was.

Chapter Twenty-Three

May 1945
Near Scheveningen and Amsterdam, The Netherlands
and Bay Ridge, Brooklyn, New York

C harlotta also was happy, and extremely relieved, to receive a telegram from Rika. It was delivered to her at the movie theater.

———◉———

GREETINGS CHARLOTTA
Staying near Scheveningen with Greta Coppens
Any news of Papa Kees Henk Bram
And our friend Lovisa
You and Bram were great to me
Please wire me back
Looking forward to seeing you again
Rika Spranger

———◉———

IT WAS FABULOUS NEWS! "One person accounted for," Charlotta exclaimed happily. "One down, four to go!"

She hurried from her office to the front of the theater where old Gerritt was behind the refreshment counter, talking to Bartol the projectionist who had emerged from his booth after starting the movie, and showed the telegram to them.

"It's from Rika! She's alive," she smiled. "Oh, thank God! Take a look."

"Rika. Is that one of the ones who was hidden here?" Bartol asked.

"Yes," Charlotta explained breezily, "Rika Spranger and her brothers. Our friends' children. But I got her out of here before the Nazis came."

"Great news," said Bartol, making the "V for victory" sign, and made his jaunty way to the men's room.

Gerritt examined the telegram. "She's in Scheveningen! Thank goodness. We could get there to see her in about an hour if the roads were passable. But look. How does Rika know about Lovisa?"

"Good question," Charlotta said. "Sounds like we're not the only ones to be worried about your niece."

"What's this about a niece?" Betje, who was coming back from the ladies' lounge during a lull in ticket buyers, sidled over to them, butted in, and asked.

"Lovisa," Gerritt replied.

"Oh, yes, that's your friend, right?" Betje asked Charlotta. She couldn't help it. More jealousy surged up within her as she thought of how close Lovisa and Charlotta had become over the last few years. Lovisa, the friend who replaced her. She was always coming into the theater, always going off into the back office to talk to Charlotta, and they always talked alone.

Always excluding her.

"She's my niece," Gerritt explained softly.

"She's your *what?*" Betje repeated. She also blanched. Gerritt's niece? This wasn't the answer she had expected. She had always liked Gerritt but loathed Lovisa.

They couldn't be related.

They just couldn't.

But apparently, they were.

"She's also a member of the Resistance who helped find hiding places for Rika Spranger and my son, Nikolaas," added Charlotta, watching Betje carefully. Why was she looking so shocked? Her eyes were wider than saucers, and not with pleasant surprise, either.

More like she was angry.

"Never knew you, ahem, had a niece," Betje mumbled to Gerritt.

"That's because she didn't come around here too much before the occupation started, but once it did, we didn't want to advertise our association," Gerritt explained. "She was extremely active in helping to hide people. You know how the Nazis were. If she had been caught, and they found out I was her uncle, I might have been hauled in for interrogation. Lovisa didn't want that to happen and said so. Many, many times." Gerritt explained.

"So you kept her a secret?" Betje asked.

"Yes. I behaved, whenever I saw her here, like she was just another patron, and not my only brother's daughter," Gerritt said.

"She's still unaccounted for. It's not good. It's been almost a week since the ceasefire and there's been no sign of her. But we just got word," Charlotta continued, "Rika's alive! Rika Spranger. In hiding in Scheveningen. We had her hidden here in the theater for a while, too."

"*She* was one of the two people you had in hiding, here? But I thought whoever you'd hidden were found on the day of the raid," Betje said, which would have meant they were all transported away by the Nazis, and probably would not be returning to the Netherlands, either. "How did she get to Scheveningen, then?"

Betje had also assumed Charlotta and Bram had been protecting adults. Not a teenage girl.

Certainly not the kindhearted teenage girl who had, years ago, always greeted Betje with such a beautiful smile, and also had always been so welcoming to her daughter, Lisette.

"She and her brothers were in hiding here," explained Charlotta, "all three of them. I got Rika out of here right before the raid that found the boys. The *vieze honden* only found two, as a result," she added, calling the Nazis dirty dogs. "They didn't get all three."

Betje almost keeled over. She felt as though she had just been punched in the gut. All three *Spranger children* had been hidden *here*?

At that point, Betje seemed to back away from Gerritt and Charlotta.

Odd, Charlotta thought.

"I, I, I'm – sorry, I think I'm going to be sick," Betje stammered, and all but ran right back to the ladies' lounge.

"That one! She's been acting strangely ever since the war started," Gerritt commented, shaking his head.

"She has, has she?" Charlotta asked.

"Yes, she's been very, I don't know, watchful all the time," Gerritt told her, relieved to finally mention it.

"We all were in those days, though, weren't we?"

"*Ja,* but that was to avoid the Nazis. This, this was, I don't know how to explain it. Something else." Gerritt paused for a moment before adding, "She seemed to pay a little too much attention *to you*, Charlotta."

For the moment, Charlotta could only wonder about whatever was behind that.

But it was setting off alarm bells in her head, and she planned to get to the bottom of it.

———— ◉ ————

BETJE REALLY DID GET sick once she ran into the bathroom. She wasn't bluffing when she said she didn't feel well.

She hadn't known it was the three Spranger teenagers who had been in hiding in the building. Somehow or other she had been under the impression it had been adults, with fancy careers, like university professors or something. People who could afford to pay to be hidden.

Not the Sprangers.

And so far only one of them had survived.

It couldn't have been more horrible.

———— ◉ ————

ANOTHER TELEGRAM ARRIVED at the theater for Charlotta later that same day. This one was from Florentine.

———⬤———

MORE GRATEFUL TO YOU than I can
   ever express for hiding my children
   Bravo
   Oranje boven
   Love Florentine and Reenie and Billy

———⬤———

CHARLOTTA SMILED AT that at first, but who were Reenie and Billy?

It took her a few seconds before she realized those must be Verena and Willem's nicknames.

Rika must have wired Florentine about the help she'd received from Charlotta.

Then she sighed.

Yes, she had assisted the Spranger children, and done so willingly to try to save their lives, but the results had been catastrophic. Two of them were caught. So was Bram.

What would Florentine think when she heard that sordid part of the story? Just how grateful might she be then, when she heard someone had reported the hiding place to the dogs of the Green Police?

It caused Charlotta to return, yet again, to the question that had been haunting her ever since the day when the hiding place had been raided, Bram and the boys seized.

Who the hell had betrayed them in the first place?

———⬤———

FATHER JOSEPHUS UNEXPECTEDLY came by Tante Greta's house a week later. The boy who'd had ten hiding places, Avram, the one Rika and Evy had brought to the parade on VE Day, was with him, as well as a twelve-year-old girl he introduced as Martine. She had been hidden at the rectory since 1942 and nobody in Father Josephus' congregation ever suspected it or knew it!

"I was," the priest winked at Rika, "more involved in the Resistance than you thought."

"Thank goodness for people like you," Rika smiled. She turned to the girl. "I'm really happy to meet you, Martine, and to see you again, Avram." Both of them smiled at her shyly.

Friends, she thought. I've finally got two friends who live nearby and went through variations of the same kind of wartime craziness as me.

"Shall I make all of you some tea?" Tanta Greta asked.

"That would be grand," said Father, "although after that we have to get going. I want to bring these three to the nearest Red Cross office. They can fill out the papers about their missing family members and the organization will try to trace what happened to them."

Try to trace, he'd said. Rika picked right up on the phrase, knowing what it said, but also what it didn't. Those who would try might not be able to succeed.

Not in all instances. Maybe not even in most.

But it might turn out to be worth it.

———◉———

IF THE SCHEVENINGEN office was any indication, the tracing service at the Red Cross had an enormous, major job on its hands. There were at least forty people in line ahead of Father, Avram, Martine and Rika, and those were just the ones in Scheveningen. The organization had offices all over Holland and Rika guessed they were just as crowded.

It wasn't just Jews who were looking for their lost family members, either. The Germans had seized so many Dutch people for forced labor that their relatives needed help finding out where they were, too.

While they waited on the line, Rika noticed a sign hanging on a nearby wall. It said HELP WANTED.

That got her thinking. She was seventeen, almost eighteen. She wanted to stay with Tante Greta for the time being, but it wasn't a good idea to remain there without supporting herself. Not at this age. If she could work for the tracing service, she would also be able to get information about her father, brothers and Bram faster than she might if she waited around for it.

"Father," she said to the priest, "I want to apply to work here and help."

"That," he replied, "is an astonishingly great idea."

"It looks like they're going to need you," little Martine agreed, as they continued to wait on the line.

Chapter Twenty-Four

June 1945

Near Scheveningen, Amsterdam and Brooklyn

Florentine's new mission in life was to get her daughter onto a ship. She wanted Rika to sail to the United States as soon as possible.

As glad as she was that her daughter had been hidden and survived, when she thought twice about it, Florentine was mad, too. She had no issue with Charlotta or this other woman, Greta Coppens, who had hidden her, in fact she wanted to give them a medal for helping Rika, but she wished she could slay whatever Nazis had passed so many decrees against Jewish people in the first place that her poor girl had had no choice but to live underground, like a criminal, until the regime was over.

Word spread outward from the flower shop that Rika was alive and well, and the people of Brooklyn seemed to rejoice right alongside of Florentine, Reenie and Billy. There was a steady parade of both old and new customers who stopped by to congratulate them.

Florentine believed they had been lucky to resettle in Brooklyn in more ways than just one. They'd landed in a warmhearted borough of really terrific people in this part of New York City. Monty brought Reenie and Billy out for ice cream sundaes on the day after they'd gotten the good news. An Irish family that usually came into the shop to order decorations for their dead grandparents' graves even showed up bearing a chocolate cake. "This is to help you celebrate, Mrs. Spranger," the eldest daughter said as she gave it to her.

One sweet-faced young mother showed up to say congratulations, too, but with tears in her eyes. "I am from Stuttgart," she said. "Jewish.

My name is Rachelle. We haven't had any word of my sisters, brothers, nieces and nephews at all."

"It's early yet," Florentine said to her kindly, her heart going out to the woman. "Don't give up hope."

"Hope? What's that?" The woman replied.

Florentine knew exactly what she meant. "Three members of my family are still missing, too. Right now all I can think about is getting my daughter a passage here."

A day later that same woman, Rachelle, came back into the shop. She still looked miserable about her own family situation, but handed Florentine a piece of paper with a name and a phone number written on it. "My husband," she said, "works for the State Department. He can help you get your daughter here."

Florentine thanked her with a bunch of lilacs and roses.

———————◉———————

NIKOLAAS WAS BACK!

Emmi could hardly believe it when she opened the door to the apartment and found her brother standing there.

"Emmi!" He shouted happily, picking her up and swinging his little sister, who was no longer so little, around in a circle.

"Nikolaas! Where have you been?" She asked as he put her down and followed her into the apartment.

"In Noordwijk. I was helping a woman run a tulip form. Her husband had been taken away for forced labor and she and her sister were having a tough time with the place. I couldn't do much out in the fields during the daylight hours, of course, or the *Duitsers* would have taken me, too, but I took charge of just about everything else. They had a barn with cows, horses, pigs, chickens, you name it." He patted his stomach. "I ate well. And here, I've brought these for you and Mother."

He held out a sack filled with fresh eggs. Emmi went into the kitchen, removed a large bowl from the cupboard, and carefully put the eggs into it.

"She's going to be so happy to see you," Emmi told him as she worked. "We've had lots of good news about Rika. She made it! She's working in Scheveningen with the Red Cross Tracing Service, can you believe it? But she's the only one, so far. And now you! Honestly, Nikolaas, Mother and I were afraid you were never coming back."

"It wasn't easy getting here over some of the torn-up roads. And I'm only staying with you for a few days," her brother explained. "I want to go back and keep working on the farm until, I mean if, the husband returns."

"Oho! Sweet on the wife, then, are you?" Emmi teased.

"You could always read me like a book, kid! Yes. Her name is Grietje and I love her very much, though she doesn't know it yet."

"Really? I have a feeling she might have already figured it out," grinned Emmi. "Oh, it's wonderful to see you!"

And to know he was alive, not dead.

She hugged her brother again.

───────◉───────

THE NEXT EVENING WAS a jolly night at the Van Der Graaf apartment, for a change.

For one thing, the fresh eggs provided for an astonishingly good dinner, supplemented by some carrots Charlotta had managed to secure on the black market.

For another, Gerritt had been invited, as a thank you< since he was the one who had helped get Nikolaas and Rika get out of town in the first place by putting them on to Lovisa in the first place.

Emmi wished Rika could have joined them, too, but she was busy working. It had been years since she'd seen her. She hadn't even known her parents were hiding her, along with her brothers, until about a year after her father Bram's arrest, when her mother finally told her the full truth about what happened.

On the other hand, she was glad that Rika was working at the tracing service, because maybe she could find out something about Bram.

It didn't look good for him, though. The country had been liberated for a month, and so far, no Bram.

The talk after dinner turned to the question of who had betrayed them back in 1942. Gerritt brought it up because he was still waiting for any kind of news whatsoever about Lovisa.

"I can't help but wonder," he revealed to them, "if it's all connected somehow. The theater is where Rika, Henk and Kees were hiding, and later, Lovisa was using it as a message drop for the Resistance."

"She was?" Emmi asked, awestruck at the idea.

"She certainly was," said Charlotta. "With my permission."

"Wow. How did that work?" Nikolaas wanted to know.

"It was carried out in the ladies' room," Charlotta told them. "There was a loose tile on the floor that could easily be pulled up. She'd leave a message underneath it, on a small scrap of paper, like on brown paper from a bag. The message was always written in invisible ink, so if anybody except the courier who was there to retrieve the message managed to find it, it just looked like a little sliver of garbage." She laughed. "But it sure wasn't!"

"Ingenious," Gerritt said.

"Do you really think somehow the two, shall we say, *extra uses* of the theater might have been linked?" Nikolaas asked him. "I don't see any connection between hiding people and dropping messages."

"Me neither," said Emmi.

"Unless," Gerritt explained quietly, "the same informer betrayed them all. Bram, Kees, Henk, and later, Lovisa."

"Was Lovisa betrayed too?" Emmi asked.

"We aren't sure," said Gerritt. "But I would assume so. It isn't like her to just disappear and not get any word to me. She wouldn't do that unless she *couldn't*, for whatever the reason. So I have to question what went on. She must have been arrested toward the end of the war, and now she hasn't surfaced yet. That's what makes me think she could have been picked up by the Green Police or the Gestapo."

Nikolaas shook his head, remembering how enchanting a gal Lovisa had been when he met her. He hoped she wasn't lying dead somewhere, dispatched by the Gestapo.

"Let's get to the heart of this matter," Emmi suggested, "although using the word *heart* maybe isn't the best way to describe it. Who could have been the betrayer? We don't know yet if there was one where Lovisa was concerned, so first, who might have informed on the boys?"

"Corina Temmink," her mother replied at once. "She must have known something about it since she lived right next door to the theater and her daughters made snide remarks to you."

"I remember," Emmi sighed. "And I asked Paolo about it, before the Germans shipped him off."

"You did?" Charlotta asked. "Why in the world did you ask him? Not that he didn't seem trustworthy or anything. I just wish you hadn't done it."

"I didn't think you or Papa would tell me the truth," Emmi explained, "but Paolo, I figured if it was happening at the theater, he'd know. Nikolaas came that day and brought me out for ice cream right after I talked to Paolo, though, and then Gerritt, you came to warn Nikolaas about the raid. I doubt Paolo had time to spread the word."

"You never know, though," said Charlotta. "I still wonder if it wasn't Corina. She's my likeliest suspect. She was even sleeping around with the Nazis, so let's face it, that woman was capable of anything."

"And then wasn't there a drunk who fell asleep in the theater one night and saw the kids when they came out of their hiding places?" Nikolaas said.

"Yes," Charlotta admitted sadly.

"There was?" Emmi asked, wide-eyed.

"Yes, a very unpleasant drunk," her mother told her. "One look at the boys and he pegged them as Jewish. Kees called us here and your father broke curfew to run right over to the theater. He tried to straighten the matter out with the man, offered him more drinks, movie passes and everything. Your father wasn't sure if it would be enough or not. Next afternoon we were raided. I wonder where he is now, that awful man. Hannus Douw."

Emmi gasped. "Hannus Douw! I know who he is!"

Everyone gaped at her. "Where," Charlotta asked, "did you ever meet the likes of him?"

"At Lisette's," she replied. "He's dating her mother."

"He's stepping out with Betje?" Charlotta gasped.

Emmi replied, "Yes!"

"She never mentioned it," Charlotta said with a shake of her head. She'd grown a lot less close to Betje since the war began, but even so. Betje used to come on the run to tell her every time a man so much as glanced in her direction. Why hadn't she mentioned Hannus Douw?

Was it perhaps because she and Hannus Douw had been involved in the betrayal *together?*

"How long has that been going on?" Emmi's brother asked her.

"Ages and ages! Since, oh, I guess, around the time of the raid," Emmi relayed.

"And Betje, of course, has access to the ladies' room at the theater," said Gerritt slowly, "where she might have noticed something going on with the tile. And Lovisa."

"I had the feeling that Betje really didn't like it that I was friendly with Lovisa," Charlotta said. "But would she have reported Bram, the boys, and Lovisa, just out of stupid jealousy?"

"I would say," said Gerritt, "that's entirely possible."

"I never liked her much," Emmi revealed. "I was never sure why. I didn't mind her daughter Lisette, though she's never really been one of my favorite people, but Betje? She just always gave me a bad feeling."

"If she had anything to do with all this," Charlotta declared, "I'm going to give her a worse feeling!"

That was when there was a knock on their apartment door.

"Who can this be?" Charlotta asked as she got up to answer it.

When she did, she couldn't believe what she saw.

The man was as thin as a pipe cleaner. He looked decimated and weary, but she'd know him anywhere by his beautiful blue eyes.

"*Bram!*" She exclaimed joyfully. "Emmi, Nikolaas, Gerritt, it's Bram! He's home!"

That ended the speculations about the identity of the betrayer, at least for that night.

———— ◉ ————

RIKA RECOGNIZED THE name of the man who had come to sit before her desk at the Red Cross.

She had never seen his face before, but she knew who he was as soon as she looked at the sheet of information he had filled out about his missing uncle from Scheveningen.

"Gustav De Boon," she read out loud. "It says on here you're a projectionist from Amsterdam. Well, believe it or not, I know who you are, even if you've never seen me before and we haven't officially met."

"How's that?" Gustav asked her.

So this was Gustav! His hair was bright red, his eyes gray. A rather plain man. Heavyset. No wonder he'd made such a racket while going up and down the stairs.

"I was hidden for months in the Van Der Graaf's theater," Rika replied. "In a tiny room right across from your projectionist's booth."

"Good God," Gustav breathed. "Seriously?"

"You think I could make that up?" Rika grinned. The longer she worked, the more the sunny personality she'd once had started to emerge again. She enjoyed talking to people, hearing their stories, and trying to help them.

"You've got to be making it up," Gustav replied with a laugh, figuring this was a big joke.

"Oh really?" She countered. "How's your girlfriend Marijke?"

"What?" He repeated, taken aback. "How do you know about her?"

"I just told you. I was hidden in the room across from where you worked. On the weekend shift. You only worked weekends."

"This is unbelievable," Gustav breathed. "The way I heard it, the boss was hiding people in the theater and they got them."

"Not all of them. I'm living proof. So really, how is Marijke? The two of you were sitting right outside my door one time, on the floor, I guess, sharing a bottle of alcohol."

"I remember that! I had to break up with her. During the week I worked at my grandfather's restaurant. She came storming in there at one point saying Jews were being hidden in the theater. She was shouting it loudly, and in front of all the patrons. At first I didn't believe it. Next thing I heard, the boss had been arrested, there really had been Jews there, and they were caught along with the boss. I think she might even have been the one who turned them in." He hung his head. "If she did, it was my fault. I was always sneaking her into the theater. Sometimes she wandered around the place. I don't know how she knew, but she did."

Had Marijke really been the one? Rika would have to pass this along to Charlotta when she saw her in Amsterdam. She was planning a trip up there that coming weekend, now that Bram was home.

"There were two boys hiding there besides me," Rika said. "They were my brothers. We don't know yet what happened to them."

Gustav felt even worse.

He almost gave this pretty girl Marijke's current address but stopped himself just in time.

On the one hand, if Marijke's actions had caused two boys to be sent to those awful camps, that was about the worst thing anyone ever could have done.

But on the other, if those boys were already dead, they were dead. What good would it do if he gave this girl the information of where to find Marijke?

"I hope you find your brothers," is all he could manage to say.

Chapter Twenty-Five

June 1945
Amsterdam

No new information about Kees or Henk had come in before Rika boarded a bus for Amsterdam on Friday right after work.

Just the day after Gustav De Boon had shown up in her office, there had finally been news about her father, Julius. After his arrest he had been sent to a camp. One of the worst ones. Rika didn't even want to acknowledge its name.

Julius, the father she adored, didn't make it. He died a few months after arriving at the camp.

In a way the news was to be expected. He had been taken back in 1942. The prisoners who had first been selected to work in those awful concentration camps didn't last very long.

Papa's name was found on a list of the dead. Rika had asked the director of her office to please be the one to notify her mother, too upset to be able to send the cable herself.

That poor, good man.

Her Papa.

But although Rika hadn't had the heart to contact her mother with the devastating news, her mother didn't hesitate to get in touch with her, and immediately. The next day Florentine sent her a wire.

It said:

―――――――•◉•―――――――

SO SORRY NOT TO BE there when you received the sad news. Papa loved and adored you Rika. Our job now is to do him proud.

I love you, too.

Mama

Rika felt better as soon as she read it.

Henk and Kees were still missing, but she hadn't given up on them yet. Maybe, she told herself, just maybe, there's still a chance I'll see my brothers again. It was beginning to look more and more unlikely, but even so. Bram was alive, and that hadn't really seemed very probable, either.

Now here she was, on her way to see him and his wife.

Rika settled into a worn-out seat on the bus, which, like everything and everybody else following the long war, had seen better days, and forced herself to try and just enjoy the view.

———— ◉ ————

BRAM LOOKED LIKE HE was only a few pounds heavier than a skeleton, but his face lit up the second he saw Rika.

"My wonderful girl," he proclaimed as he gave her a weak hug. "Seeing you here, standing before us, makes it all worth it."

There were hugs and kisses from Charlotta, Nikolaas and Emmi, too. Nikolaas had come to visit, bearing more eggs, Charlotta had gotten her hands on potatoes, and they were having a fine dinner.

"Have I ever missed you," Emmi told her.

"I missed you, too. All of you," Rika said with emotion. "And I can't thank you enough for everything." She had brought four jars of the jam she and Tante Greta liked to make and gave it to Charlotta.

"You don't have to thank us," said Charlotta warmly, "helping you was doing the right thing, and that's all there was to it."

"Oh, I'd say there was a lot more to it," Rika said, making the others laugh.

She told them, haltingly, about her father. After that, she changed the subject away from Papa as fast as she could, telling Bram she wanted to hear all about where he had been sent.

He told her he'd been forced into an actual work camp, not a death camp. It made ammunition for the Nazis. "My job was, I had to load the gunpowder into the bullets," he said. Then he grinned. "But don't worry. I sabotaged as many of them as possible by not quite loading them enough."

Rika said that was not just gutsy but great.

Then she told them her other news. "Your projectionist, Gustav De Boon. He wound up in my office," she began. For the first time she told them about how he had sneaked Marijka into the theater, and his theory that she may have been the informant. "She apparently announced that you were hiding us to Gustav's grandfather's whole restaurant."

Charlotta gasped at that.

"I thought you figured it was Corina, Mama," Emmi piped up, popping a forkful of potato into her mouth.

"Oh, no," Bram spoke up. "It wasn't Corina at all."

Everyone stopped eating and looked at him.

"I had some freedom of movement at my camp," he explained. "They gave me a position of responsibility, had me supervising some of the other forced laborers in my division. That's how every now and again I got to sabotage some of the bullets. I was the one who inspected them and gave them a pass, you see. I'd say they were all up to standard but some of them always weren't. Anyway as the situation deteriorated at the end of the war, and the Germans who ran the place fled, in the chaos I managed to have a look at my file."

"Well don't keep us in suspense," Nikolaas said. "Who is the creep that did it? Hannus Douw?"

"Corina Teemink?" Charlotta asked.

"Her daughters, Lena and Neeltje?" Rika tried.

Bram shook his head. "None of them. Believe it or not, the informer was little Lisette Van Beek. Betje's daughter."

"Lisette!" Emmi exclaimed. "But she's my friend!"

"Betje's daughter?" Charlotta repeated wearily. "Oh, good God in heaven. Why?"

"She would only have been what, eleven?" Rika asked.

Emmi, Nikolaas and Rika exchanged glances. They knew they would have to confront her.

"We'll find out," Nikolaas said. "Tomorrow."

"What's wrong with tonight?" Charlotta asked, standing up and taking command. She had never felt more furious in her life. Lisette! *Unbelievable!* "I'm going to ask the two of them to come over here right now. They still live in this building."

She marched over to the telephone and summoned them both, somehow keeping her voice level. "Betje, why don't you come over and bring Lisette? Rika's here, Bram's back, Nikolaas showed up, and we're having a little gathering."

That was one way of describing it.

This was a showdown.

———— ⊙ ————

BETJE WONDERED WHAT had brought on the invitation to the Van Der Graaf's. She couldn't remember the last time her friend had asked her over, but wasn't going to hesitate.

"Come on, Lisette," she called to her daughter, "there's a party at the Van Der Graaf's."

"Do I have to go there?" Lisette whined. "Don't I see enough of Emmi at school?"

"They've asked for us both. Just come along and don't be so stubborn," Betje urged her. "Maybe they've got treats."

Lisette made a face but said all right. She was always up for something good to eat.

Betje figured they'd be walking into a lovely congenial atmosphere among old friends and soon all would be well between her and Charlotta again.

Was she ever wrong.

First she was shocked when Charlotta opened the door to her knock and looked at the two of them with fire in her eyes.

"Come in," Charlotta said in a cold, clipped tone. "Sit down. There's much to discuss."

Betje was baffled. "Discuss?"

Lisette was scared. She knew she shouldn't have done it. Not when the news about the true nature of the concentration camps had come out.

But there was no way they could know what she did.

Was there?

Apparently there was.

"We know it was you, Lisette," Bram informed her.

"What was her?" Betje asked.

"We know," Charlotta said through gritted teeth, "that *your daughter* informed on my husband for hiding Rika and her brothers in the theater."

Lisette found it was hard to breathe.

"What do you mean? Are you calling my child an informant?" Betje demanded. "What are you people saying, and who do you think you are? My child isn't an informant! My daughter would never, ever do anything even remotely like what you're suggesting, and - "

"You can stop right there. Your daughter," Bram continued with steely calm, "was named as the informant in my case. I saw the file. Her name was written in it, Lisette Van Beek, so the two of you would do well not to bother trying to deny it."

"We already know it was you, Lisette," Rika all but spat.

"Why?" Charlotta demanded of the child.

"But there's nothing to this," Betje tried to interject. Or was there?

"There certainly is," retorted Nikolaas, "and this is serious. Kees and Henk still aren't back. They might have been killed, and if they were, it's because Lisette jumped into the middle of this, interfered, and caused all kinds of trouble. And her actions are also what brought my father here to within an inch of losing his life by starving in a camp, too."

Lisette started to cry. "I was just trying to help!" She protested.

"Help who?" Her appalled mother asked, finding all of this hard to believe, yet shocked to the core at her daughter's admission.

"Help you!" Lisette sobbed. "You were always complaining! Charlotta didn't spend time with you any longer, Charlotta was hiding something, Charlotta was up to something!"

"Oh, merciful God," Betje breathed, like a prayer. She really had complained an awful lot to her daughter about Charlotta when the war was going on, but what was this? What was Lisette saying? She'd turned these good people in to the Nazis *for her*?

"So what did you do," Charlotta asked Lisette, looking at her with pure disgust, "spy on me?"

"I didn't have to! The Temmink girls and their mother already had. They knew there were people hidden in your building and Lena Temmink told me. Her mother told her. I just called the Green Police and passed it along to one of them."

"You *what?*" Betje roared.

"I'm sorry," Lisette cried desperately. "I didn't know what was going to happen, I just wanted to get even with you, Charlotta, because you didn't like my mother any longer, and she was driving me crazy complaining about it!"

Betje thought she might pass out. Get even? What had her daughter done?

"That's what this is about?" Nikolaas asked. "You wanted to fix your mother's friendship with mine and so you called the Nazis? Don't you know the Spranger boys might even be dead, *just because of you and your stupid phone call?*"

"I wanted to do something about the way my mother was being mistreated," Lisette told them. "I told the police it was Bram who was hiding people, not Charlotta. That was so she could get back to being a good friend to my mother again once he and the hidden Jews were out of the way."

"This is flabbergasting!" Charlotta cried. "I never mistreated your mother, Lisette! And Betje, I simply had a lot of other matters on my mind in those days than paying attention to you!"

Betje was holding her head in her hands. "I didn't mean for anything like this to happen. I didn't. No, I didn't."

"Oh, really? You brought this on, Betje," Emmi informed her.

"What are you, obsessed with my mother or something?" Nikolaas asked the woman. "That's *sick!*"

Betje didn't reply to that. The truth was that her friendship with Charlotta *had* become something of an obsession. To Betje, Charlotta had become more and more important, even vital to her well-being, especially after her husband had died, years back, of a heart attack. Charlotta had given her a job, ensuring she had a livelihood. She thought they were like sisters and always would be, but then the war got in the way.

Betje certainly had complained a lot about it to Lisette. But how had that led to this?

Rika, meanwhile, was steaming mad.

All through the war Rika had been compliant. Quiet. Willing to put up with just about anything she had to, in order to make it through.

She was not going to be quiet any longer. Lisette Van Beek, informing on her brothers and Bram! It made Rika boil. She had never before felt such white-hot rage.

"*You!*" Rika addressed Lisette. She stood up unsteadily, marched over to the cowering younger girl, stood over her, and proceeded to say, with a ton of contempt, "You ought to be locked up for this! You may have been a stupid child of eleven when it happened but you're still a traitor! A traitor! Someone who goes against your own Dutch people! Do you even realize *a fraction* of what you've done?"

"I didn't know it was your brothers," came the ridiculous little hellion's lame reply.

Rika roared, "You should be thrown in the nearest jail and never be allowed out again!"

"She's right, Lisette! You're no better than a criminal," Emmi added hotly, then pointed to Bram. "Look at my father! Just look at him! He almost starved to death in those camps, and you're the monster who put him there!"

"And you," Charlotta said, turning on Betje. "What's the other story I'm hearing regarding you and Hannus Douw?"

"What does Hannus Douw have to do with any of this?" Betje countered. "He's just a friend!"

"A friend who found my brothers and me at the theater one night, when we came out of the rooms where we hid during the day," said Rika. "He was really nasty. Sounds to me like this might be connected. Right after that, I was moved out of there, and Bram and my brothers got raided."

"We thought he was the informant," Nikolaas said.

"He heard it from me," Lisette admitted. "I told him what Neeltje and Lena Temmink had said. He said he was going to check it out himself and claim the reward that the police were paying per head whenever anybody turned in hidden people. That was when I called them first from a pay phone."

"Were you," her mother asked her dully, "planning to claim the reward before Hannus did, on top of everything else?"

"No," Lisette shrugged. "I just wanted to beat him to it."

"I can hardly," Bram exclaimed, "believe what I'm hearing! Lisette, do you know how destructive you've been?""

"Don't yell at my daughter," said Betje huffily.

"Your daughter," Charlotta informed Betje, "may have been responsible for the death of Rika's brothers. They still haven't been found yet!"

"You're fired, Betje," Bram informed her. "We did everything we could to help you when your husband died. We even gave you a job. Tried our best to help because we considered you a friend. But this is as bizarre as it can get. No more! Take your pathetic excuse for a low-class piece of dung of a 'daughter' and get your ugly asses out of my apartment!"

"Yes, get out of my house," yelled Charlotta.

"We'll go with pleasure," Lisette, finally recovering from what she considered were unreasonable attacks against her, yelled back.

"I might just get all the way out of Amsterdam," Betje muttered. "Move away." She had never felt more embarrassed or ashamed, anywhere, about anything, and yanked Lisette out of the chair where the girl had been sitting. The two of them made haste to leave.

"I'm going to report you!" Rika shrieked.

Charlotta remembered something important. "Wait just one moment, Betje," she called out. She wanted her gone but had to stop her from leaving just to ask that brat of hers one more question. If she didn't ask, chances were she, Betje and Lisette would never speak again.

That request that she wait was enough to give Betje just the tiniest bit of hope. Was her Charlotta, her best friend in the world, suddenly doing an about-face, changing her mind, and calling her to come back?

But it turned out to be a whole other matter entirely.

"One more question. Lisette," Charlotta asked the girl, in a commanding voice that would brook no argument, "tell me, right now, did you inform on Lovisa, too?"

"If I did," the insufferable child roared, "I'm not telling *you!*"

"Get out," Charlotta repeated.

Rika yelled to their retreating backs, "Go live in the sewer! It's where you belong!" She strode to the door and, once Betje and Lisette had crossed the threshold, had the satisfaction of slamming the door shut with a bang behind them.

The whole group felt spent after that, all but collapsing where they sat, deflated, as if they were a bunch of balloons and the air had just been let out of them.

Rika couldn't stop shaking and neither could Charlotta. Bram had balled one hand into a fist and was hitting the open palm of the other.

Emmi was crying and put an arm around her father. "How could she do that to Papa?"

Nikolaas was inwardly raging, but he recovered first. He said, after a long pause, "That's our answer, then. It's terrible, but at least now we have the answer. We know who the informer was, a twisted little girl with a strange as hell mother, and we won't ever have to wonder about it any further."

"She wouldn't admit to betraying Lovisa," Rika said dully.

"Who was also doing something against the regime at our theater," Charlotta told the others, and explained to her about the tile on the ladies' room floor and the secrets that were concealed beneath it.

"We should report the Temminks, too," suggested Nikolaas. "This filtered down to Lisette from Corina and her daughters."

"And Douw," said Bram. "He was in on this, too. The bum."

"I second both ideas," agreed Rika. "Douw pushed Lisette along, but this seems like it all started with the Temmink mother."

"Whose head was shaved in the street on VE Day for sleeping with the Nazis," Emmi told her. "You missed it, Rika. Wasn't that a sight!"

"Yes," agreed Charlotta, finally managing a little smile. "*Boontje komt om zijn loontje.*" The little bean gets what it deserves.

In other words, what goes around, comes around.

Chapter Twenty-Six

Scheveningen, Netherlands and Brooklyn, New York
July 1945

———————◆———————

RIKA WAS GLAD TO GET back to Scheveningen.

As grand as it had been to see the Van Der Graafs again, the revelations made by that atrocious girl, Lisette, had left her reeling. It was hard to fathom just what had gone on in the stupid little idiot's head if she thought that by reporting poor Bram, and informing on Rika's own wonderful brothers, it would bring Charlotta closer to her mother. What kind of backwards logic was that? The whole idea was crazy.

And the mother, Betje. She was some type of a lunatic, too, in Rika's opinion. Something wrong there.

How many times must that woman have moaned to Lisette about the big "problem" of her fractured friendship with Charlotta?

Had she really pushed the girl over the edge with that subject, to the point Lisette made that phone call to the Green Police?

Wasn't it also bizarre that Betje had been so obsessed with Charlotta in the first place?

It was one of those wartime acts of malevolence that Rika might never be able to figure out or understand.

So she was relieved to be back at the Red Cross office, speaking with the relatives of the missing and the lost. So many of them had incredible stories. Her family wasn't the only one affected by an informant, but Lisette's motivations for her actions were probably among the strangest ones in Europe.

At least there had been one good thing to happen during her visit to the Van Der Graafs. The little hat that her mother had bought for her back before leaving for America had been found! She had accidentally left it behind when she stayed there, in her old apartment, right before being moved on to Evy's and then Tante Greta's. She had it back at last.

Later that afternoon, one of the directors of the office, Hendrik, came over to Rika's desk.

He was smiling.

He was also holding a piece of paper up like it was a trophy.

"Here's something you might want to see," he told her, and handed the piece of paper over.

It was a letter from someplace called the 131st Evacuation Hospital near Mauthausen in Austria, and it had been addressed to Hendrik.

Rika found her heart was pounding in her chest. Could it be?

She began to read.

———◉———

WITH REGARD TO YOUR inquiry as to the Dutch nationals Henk and Kees Spranger, I am very pleased to inform you they are patients recovering here since Liberation, and will soon be ready for release...

———◉———

THAT WAS ALL RIKA READ.

It was all she really needed to read.

She could hardly believe it.

It was against all the odds.

She had even begun to believe that ever seeing a letter such as the one she was holding right now in her hands would prove to be impossible.

But it wasn't!

She jumped up from her seat and announced to the whole office, "It's my brothers! They're *alive!*"

———◉———

IT WAS MONTY THE TELEGRAM messenger who delivered the good news to Florentine, Billy and Reenie again.

He had grown closer to this terrific Dutch family over the last few weeks. He and Reenie were going out on dates. He not only knew Florentine had gotten the sad news that her husband had died but had gone to the short service for Julius at the synagogue. He knew there were two Spranger sons that were still unaccounted for.

He wasn't the only Brooklyn friend of the Sprangers who had been praying for news of those boys. Most of the floral shop's customers were sending appeals heavenward from synagogues. Lots of candles had even been lit at the nearest Catholic church for Florentine and her family.

The telegram came from Scheveningen again, so Monty had hope that this was it.

He also braced himself. It could just as easily have contained good news as the bad kind, the news that would break the family's heart.

"Hi," he said to Florentine, who was sorting carnations by color on a counter. "Telegram."

Florentine took it from his hand and opened it. "Oh," she said as she read, all but swooning. She steadied herself with one hand on the counter while still holding the telegram with the other. "Oh, my, Monty! Oh, my!"

"What does it say?" He couldn't resist asking.

"Henk and Kees, my boys, they're in a hospital, in Austria, *alive!*"

She started to cry, and Monty found there were tears in his eyes, too.

"Where's Reenie and Billy?" He asked.

"Two doors down, having pizza and a soda," Florentine said. "Monty, would you do me a favor and go get them?"

"I sure would!"

Monty went to the pizzeria and found the brother and sister sitting in a booth and laughing. Billy had a comic book, and Reenie was looking through a movie magazine.

"You might want to finish up and go back to the shop," Monty said to them. He tried to keep a straight face but it didn't work. Monty was all smiles.

"How come?" Billy asked.

"Go and see," Monty replied.

The siblings exchanged a look.

Within a second they were up on their feet and rushing out of the pizza place.

Monty followed them back into the flower shop. What a sight! Mother, son and daughter had joined hands and were jumping up and down and dancing in a little circle.

"Soon," Florentine was saying, as she went to the refrigerator to get a bottle of ginger ale and poured some into cups for the four of them. "We're going to get them here as soon as we can!"

"When?" Reenie and Billy asked in unison.

"The minute the boys are well enough to travel, we can get them visas, and away from Europe they go!" Smiled Florentine. Then she added, "What am I saying? Boys? One is nineteen and the other one's twenty!"

"And Rika's going to be eighteen soon," Reenie added. "In two more weeks."

"If only I could get them here in time for her birthday," sighed Florentine. "Oh, well. We'll do what we can. Cheers!"

The four of them raised their cups of soda and clinked glasses.

Chapter Twenty-Seven

Rotterdam, The Netherlands and New York City
December 1945

———————◦———————

IT WASN'T UNTIL DECEMBER, right after the first postwar Hanukkah, that everything was set for their departure.

The Netherlands had begun bouncing back, slowly but surely, from the destructiveness of the war. The port in Rotterdam was operational again. On an overcast day in early December, Henk, Kees and Rika Spranger boarded the ship that would take them to the United States of America, and more than that, to their mother, brother, sister, and their new home.

The Van Der Graafs came to see them off.

So did Evy and her parents, and Tante Greta and Father Josephus, along with Avram and Martine.

And so did Lovisa.

As it turned out, right before the war ended, she had been tipped off that the Gestapo was about to arrest her. If they had, she probably would have been given the death penalty for her list of "crimes" against the Nazis, or shot on the spot.

It didn't matter that she had been guilty of anything other than helping to save lives, which would not have been considered a criminal offense anywhere else. Under the illogical Nazi system, what she had done went against their rules, and that made her a transgressor of the worst order.

She had managed to get away from Amsterdam the same way she'd spirited Rika out of there, on a barge that ran from the Amstelkanaal to the Amstel River. She had stayed with friends on a farm until the war ended.

She'd also managed to break a leg, and hadn't returned home until she got rid of her crutches.

Lisette hadn't had a hand in informing on her at all.

Betje and Lisette had moved out of their apartment by September. The Van Der Graafs had no idea where they went, nor did they care to find out.

Rika would always wonder how in the world misguided Lisette could live with herself.

Henk and Kees had come back to Holland thinner and frailer, but were still the same wonderful brothers that Rika remembered, and they were getting better all the time. The two of them had been sent, initially, to a camp associated with an airplane factory, where they had managed to stay for most of the war. It wasn't one of those camps with the gas chambers.

As the Russians and Americans began to push the Germans back, though, the boys had been forced to march Mauthausen in Germany, another wretched camp. Conditions were terrible, with almost no food, plenty of diseases, sadistic guards, the works.

But Henk and Kees hung on and made it to see the day of liberation. Shortly thereafter they were both moved to a hospital to recover from the years of deprivation and starvation.

Once they were released, they temporarily moved in with Rika and Tante Greta, where they had a chance to build themselves back up again and get stronger. They even helped Rika plant a new flower garden for Tante Greta.

Rika would have felt terrible about leaving Tante Greta in her mansion all alone, but Father Josephus had figured out a fine way to solve that problem. Avram's father had returned from deportation, but Little Martine's family hadn't. She was all alone, too, so she moved in with Tante Greta. Tante was already looking into adopting her. Besides, her son, who had been in England with the Dutch Army in exile since the war began, would soon be coming back home, and he'd be living there again, too.

These fabulous people who had been such a special part of their lives stood on the pier and waved goodbye as the sleek ship pulled away.

Onboard the ship, the three siblings began to make up for a lot of the fun they'd missed, and also started to remember how to just relax. There was plenty of food, bands playing dance music, games like shuffleboard, strolls around the deck, and time they could simply spend outside, bundled up against the December wind on their deck chairs, just watching the sapphire waves of the Atlantic Ocean.

———————— ● ————————

GETTING TO NEW YORK took them fifteen days. After sailing past the Statue of Liberty, they had to be examined at Ellis Island to make sure they were medically fit to enter the country, and even after the boys' long ordeal, somehow they had managed to pass with flying colors.

After that, the passengers were finally brought to the pier in New York. Rika was wearing the hat her mother had given her so long ago, the white one with the light blue trim.

The terminal was huge. They found their baggage under a banner bearing the letter S that was hanging from the ceiling and could not help but wonder how they were ever going to find their mother in the midst of so many disembarking passengers.

But then Rika saw it.

So did Kees. "There!" He pointed.

"Yes, there she is," Henk said, beginning to smile.

Right away, Rika had recognized her mother! "She's got a sign," she added excitedly.

Florentine was accompanied by a small contingent of people. They were holding up a long banner.

The three siblings began to walk across the terminal towards them. If the place wasn't so crowded they would have broken into a run.

Yes, there was their mother! Standing beside her was a boy and girl who could only be Verena and Willem. Rika knew, from the letters that had been flying back and forth between the family members, that they now called themselves "Reenie" and "Billy," American nicknames. Wow, she thought as she continued to cross the terminal floor, they were six years older, and so much taller than they had been the last time she'd seen them, but she recognized them immediately anyway. Both were not just holding up the banner but jumping up and down with enthusiasm at the same time.

Another boy was there as well. They'd soon learn that he was Monty, Reenie's sweetheart.

A woman called Rachelle and her husband, both of whom had helped to cut through a lot of red tape to get the Sprangers to New York as fast as possible, were also present, and so was Celeste Mancini, their mother's assistant, and her two children.

They got close enough to read what was on the homemade banner. It proclaimed:

RIKA, HENK & KEYS,
WELCOME TO NEW YORK
WHERE YOU'LL BLOOM LIKE THREE TULIPS!

Suddenly Florentine was there, taking Rika into her arms, and then reaching for her sons. Billy ran to Henk, Reenie to Kees. The other smiling people holding up the banner, the new friends they hadn't met yet, reached out, one by one, shook their hands, patted them on the back and kept welcoming them to America.

"Do you like the sign?" Reenie asked her sister once she made her way over to Rika and hugged her. "It was my idea, from what you said in that terrific first telegram we received from you."

"I sure do like it! I *love* it! And I absolutely can't wait to start blooming like a tulip." And then, remembering the Nazi attempt to kick a certain royal Dutch color out of the rainbow, she added, "So long as it's an *orange* one!"

————●————

THE END

Author's Note

HELLO THERE AND GREETINGS from New York City!

Thank you so much for reading TO BLOOM LIKE A TULIP. It was an intriguing historical mystery to write.

I hope you have enjoyed reading this story about good people struggling to live through a dark time, and if you have, please be an absolute darling and leave a book review on sites like Goodreads, or wherever booksellers and book lovers meet online. You can't imagine how much your reviews and ratings can help authors. We love our happy reviewers!

I have long been intrigued by the experiences of people, especially the civilians, who lived through World War II in Europe and Asia, where the Nazi and Japanese occupiers turned their ordinary lives upside down. Soldiers are trained to fight on battlefields; civilians are not, but were swept up in the conflicts of their regions anyway. The persecuted Jewish people during the abominable Third Reich didn't ask to be targets of the Nazis, but they were, and had to find ways of surviving.

My knowledge of this time period was greatly enhanced by my friendship with Johanna Reiss, hidden child, Dutch Holocaust survivor, and Newbery Award-winning Author of the beloved nonfiction book THE UPSTAIRS ROOM.

And by the way, I've said this before and will say it again, THE UPSTAIRS ROOM would make a terrific movie.

It was from Johanna that I first learned of the Nazis' absurd prohibition in Holland against the Dutch royal family's official color, orange. She also taught me how to sing the song "Oranje Boven." Johanna is ninety-two years young now, as I write this, and is slowing down, but years ago she and I could be found singing "Oranje Boven" as we walked through the streets of New York, on the way to a show, a movie, or to get some Posto's Pizza.

The rescuers of of every hidden child who made it through that awful war didn't just save their particular charges. They made it possible for them to have children and grandchildren, too. Whoever saves a life saves the world entire.

I wanted to write a mystery about hidden children whose lives during World War II, which had already been disrupted to a fare-the-well, came up against a betrayer, and had no idea who it was...but wanted to find out.

Thanks again for reading TO BLOOM LIKE A TULIP. I would welcome the chance to connect with you and hear how you liked it. You can feel free to contact me by utilizing the Contact page on my website, www.carolynsummerquinn.com[1].

Keep smiling, and whenever you possibly can, see what you can do to put a grin on somebody else's face today, too.

To life!

Love & Light, Happy Trails, & Start Blooming,

Carolyn Summer Quinn

---

1.   http://www.carolynsummerquinn.com

About Award-Winning Author
Carolyn Summer Quinn

CAROLYN SUMMER QUINN, Author of *FIFTEEN* books, Fine Art Photographer, and Winner, to date, of *FORTY-THREE* wonderful writing awards, grew up singing show tunes in "good old" Roselle and Scotch Plains, NJ, a member of an outrageous and rollicking extended family. She has a B.A. in English and Theater/Media from Kean University and now delights daily in having made her escape from the suburbs. She has lived in New York City for the past thirty-seven terrific years.

Carolyn is the Author of: two new historical novels of World War II, *To Bloom Like a Tulip* and *Until the Stars Align*; the non-fiction theatrical biography *Mama Rose's Turn,* which tells the true story of the mother of Gypsy Rose Lee; and ten delightful cozy mysteries, *Cans of Cola Just Don't Cry, The Teetotaler's Bar, There's No Cure for Impossible, The Final Comeuppance, Cloudy with a Chance of Answers, Backstabbed on Broadway, Vanished on the Vaudeville Circuit, A Charm Without a Chain, The Hollywood Backlash Moon,* and *Child of Secrets From Afar.* She has also written two books for middle-grade children, *Keep Your Songs in Your Heart* and *Now and Forevermore Arabella.* Carolyn has got an additional mystery in the works.

Carolyn says that she always tries to incorporate the message into her writing that, "You just never know what tomorrow might bring." (She freely admits she was a little over-influenced as a teen by the musical ANNIE.)

May tomorrow bring you something wonderful! You can find Carolyn Summer Quinn through her website, www.carolynsummerquinn.com[2].

---

2.   http://www.carolynsummerquinn.com

Books By Award-Winning Author
Carolyn Summer Quinn

Historical Novels:

To Bloom Like A Tulip

Until the Stars Align

Cozy Mysteries:

Cans of Cola Just Don't Cry

The Teetotaler's Bar

There's No Cure for Impossible

Child of Secrets From Afar

The Hollywood Backlash Moon

A Charm Without a Chain

Vanished on the Vaudeville Circuit

Backstabbed on Broadway

Cloudy with a Chance of Answers

The Final Comeuppance

Nonfiction Biography of a Theatrical Legend

Mama Rose's Turn: The True Story of America's
Most Notorious Stage Mother

Middle Grade Children's Books:

Now and Forevermore Arabella

Keep Your Songs in Your Heart

Don't forget to start blooming.

Milton Keynes UK
Ingram Content Group UK Ltd.
UKHW020757231024
450026UK00001B/80